伊弉冉の選択

IZANAMI'S CHOICE

選択

ADAM HEINE

BROKEN EYE BOOKS

The Hole Behind Midnight, by Clinton J. Boomer
Royden Poole's Field Guide to the 25th Hour, by Clinton J. Boomer
Crooked, by Richard Pett
Scourge of the Realm, by Erik Scott de Bie
Izanami's Choice, by Adam Heine

ANTHOLOGIES
By Faerie Light, edited by Scott Gable & C. Dombrowski
Ghost in the Cogs, edited by Scott Gable & C. Dombrowski
Tomorrow's Cthulhu, edited by Scott Gable & C. Dombrowski

www.brokeneyebooks.com
Blowing minds, one book at a time. Broken Eye Books publishes the weird side of fantasy, horror, science fiction . . . we love it all. And the blurrier the boundaries, the better.

伊弉冉の選

IZANAMI'S

CHOICE

択

ADAM HEINE

IZANAMI'S CHOICE
by ADAM HEINE
Published by
Broken Eye Books
www.brokeneyebooks.com

Cover design by Jeremy Zerfoss and Anna Romero
with kanji assistance from Brent Millis
Interior design and editing by Scott Gable, C. Dombrowski,
and Matt Youngmark

ISBN-10: 1-940372-21-6
ISBN-13: 978-1-940372-21-1

IZANAMI'S CHOICE

ADAM HEINE

AN OLDER MODEL OF *JINZOU* GUARDED THE DOOR. IT HAD A ROUNDED frame, built for form rather than function. A rough kimono covered its chassis, and someone had tied wooden sandals to its metal feet. Instead of iron artifice that moved in a mockery of human facial expression, a wooden mask sat on the droid's face, carved to look like some jovial servant, beaming at Itaru with a rictus smile. Itaru fought a shiver of disgust. Pleasant as it appeared, it was jinzou, inhuman, a created thing.

It clutched a hefty staff in one metal claw. The door behind it hung wide open, and the smell of smoke and the faint clatter of dice wafted outside. Itaru made no move to walk past the guard, even as the chubby jinzou bowed, gesturing with its free hand in the general direction of the door.

Itaru didn't bow in return. "Are you not going to invite me in?"

The droid straightened, returning its hand to its side. It scratched out in its artificial voice: "The door, sir."

"That is an invitation, ne?"

It bowed and gestured again. Then it straightened, speaking only after it had returned its hand carefully to its side. "The door, sir."

Itaru sighed. This jinzou had been cautiously trained. An invitation would make Itaru a legal guest, protected by Tokyo law. It was a common trick in *bakuto* houses and other illegal establishments. The door would be left wide open in welcome, but with no official invitation, anyone who walked through was technically a trespasser. Privately owned droids could do anything to a trespasser in their master's home.

Hayasaki Ryoma had clearly walked into this house, so Itaru had to follow. Itaru was on his last yen, hired by the powerful Hayasaki family to track the activities of Ryoma, their son. The boy was even nephew to Duke Okubo Toshimichi, the second-most important man in all of Japan. Itaru needed this job.

He touched his sleeves, reassured by the weight of his concealed *tamiken*. Carrying weapons publicly had been illegal for decades, ever since the Haito Edict in 1876, but Itaru used to be police and samurai before that. He'd carried a sword every day for nearly forty years. Damned if he was going to stop today.

He removed his shoes and entered the house. The foyer was a large, open space. A garish chandelier hung above him. The double doors across would lead to the gambling tables. To the right was a barred window—the money exchange, no doubt. A smaller, nondescript door to his left was closed.

Two large men in suits bowed graciously from the hip, entirely without suspicion. They needed none. Somewhere in this room, a glass eye had recorded Itaru's face, and other bakuto had the job of finding out who he was and whether he was an undercover cop or some other threat. He wondered how far back their records went. He had been a detective for the Tokyo Police department as recently as 1894, but that was almost eight years ago.

No, if he was in their records at all, they'd know there was no threat of him bringing police droids down on them.

He walked toward the double doors. One of the men intercepted him, pointing him toward the money exchange. "Please, sir? No spectators inside."

"Of course. So sorry." There were no droids in this room, and the barred window was carefully out of sight from the street or the jinzou out front. Gambling was illegal, and Japan's legal system considered a droid's recorded memories to be admissible evidence. Without a record of the exchange of sen for wooden tokens, no one could prove they were doing anything but playing friendly games in a private home.

Itaru traded ten sen for an equal number of wooden tokens and stepped into the main room. Tobacco saturated the air. Card and dice tables lined the walls down the entire length of the room. The dealers were mostly human, dressed in traditional kimonos. Some were barechested to display violent tattoos done in orange and black.

A single droid dealt cards near the front door. It also wore its kimono "barechested," the upper half hanging over a belt. The exposed metal frame had been meticulously painted to match the humans' tattoos. It looked up.

Itaru tensed, but it was only a glance; the dealer returned its attention to the table. Itaru forced a calming breath. *I'm too old for this* gyufun.

The players offered no surprises: factory workers, day laborers, and homeless gambling addicts trading the few sen they had for pleasure, however brief. The boy Ryoma stuck out like an outbuilding in a rice field. He sat at a dice table ten steps from the back door, the only player in the establishment wearing a European suit. He was barely twenty years old and poorly mannered; his losses were embarrassingly obvious on his glowering face.

Itaru walked the length of the room and back as though he were picky about where he wanted to play. He chose a dice table near the foyer between Ryoma and the money exchange. He sat down before he realized he'd chosen the table with the jinzou dealer.

It bowed. "Would you like to have the next roll, sir?" The jinzou spoke with a more musical tone than the droid at the door. Small components in its face moved up and down, giving the impression of an ingratiating servant.

Itaru did not bow in return. It was a struggle just to keep from sneering. Everything about the droid was incongruous, a lie, from its painted tattoos to its fake smile. The machine could tear Itaru's arms off. Jinzou were the reason Itaru had quit the police force. Eight years ago, an insubordinate droid had cost the lives of hostages in Yurakucho, yet the bust had been considered a success— hostages died, Itaru was honored, and the droid was examined and reinstated the next day.

Shortly after, Itaru took up private investigation and refused to work with jinzou again.

"No roll," he said curtly. He clacked one token onto the table and passed the dice to the player next to him.

He played slowly, betting only one token at a time no matter how much he won, keeping one eye on Ryoma. Itaru still had seven sen when the boy indecorously slammed his hands onto the gaming table. Ryoma stood abruptly and stormed to the foyer. He had no money left—Itaru had watched him lose it, chip by chip, and no coins clinked in his limp pockets.

Itaru sighed. *He's going to borrow. The boy's in debt over his head.* It was the most common story he knew. He had even told the Marquess Hayasaki, "Your son is doing what all rich, young idlers do. He spends his money on dice, drugs, and brothels, and when that runs out, he borrows against his name."

She had wanted proof, details. She paid well and Itaru needed the money, but for once, it would have been nice to be wrong.

Ryoma's voice carried through a crack in the large double doors. "I need another twenty yen."

Twenty yen! Itaru coughed and sputtered until the droid dealer had to ask him if he needed assistance. "I'm fine," he croaked. But twenty yen. That was more than Itaru could make in a season. *How deep in debt* is *that boy?*

He could not hear the exchanger's reply, but Ryoma became frantic. "You know my family, ne? Everything will be paid back!"

The exchanger muttered again, too quiet for Itaru to hear.

"A pittance!" Ryoma said. "I'll talk to my family today. You'll have it all back within a week."

The muffled response was conciliatory. A moment later, Ryoma passed by the cracked doorway, walking toward the side door across from the exchange.

Itaru knew this part of the story, too—the part where the idler's extended debts became more trouble than profit, where the usurer found more expedient ways to get a return on his investment.

One of the two men guarding the foyer stuck his head into the gambling room and shouted above the din, "Nijuni, the boss needs you."

The jinzou dealer at Itaru's table looked up and said, "Yes, sir."

Droids had to obey their masters unless it went against their hardwired directives. It settled the bets from the last roll and said, as it was ordered to, "My apologies, gentlemen. My master requires me." It left the main room through the foyer, heading in the same direction as Ryoma.

The clatter of dice made Itaru's teeth chatter. The boy was in trouble, but what could he do about it? His job was to observe.

The other players grabbed their tokens and found new tables, seemingly oblivious to Ryoma's predicament. Or maybe they knew what was going on outside and were politely ignoring it.

Itaru was hired to observe. Maybe he could get closer, confirm what he already suspected was happening, even if he couldn't do anything about it. He checked his tamiken again, collected his tokens, and made his way to the foyer.

As soon as he reached the foyer, Ryoma's outrage blared through the closed door. "Let me go! Do you have any idea who I am?"

Itaru couldn't hear the response through the closed door, but the two men in the foyer laughed.

"What's going on?" Itaru asked them.

"Keep to yourself, Uncle."

Do I help the boy? The closed door mocked him. Whether for his job or his conscience, he needed to know what was happening in there.

A thunk. Ryoma screamed.

Itaru tried a different tack. "I saw some noble runt making a fuss." He slapped his tokens onto the counter, giving a crooked grin. "Guess he's getting what he deserves, ne?"

The money exchanger chuckled. "He's paying up. His debt's longer than my pestle."

They laughed. Itaru collected his sen from the man behind the counter, forcing a laugh too.

"Boy's a fool," said one of the guards. "His name's worth eight times what he owes, and the boss is tired of sucking up to him."

"So it's ransom?" Itaru said. He saw a glint of suspicion, so he quickly shrugged and added, "More than he deserves, I say. What if they don't pay?"

"It's their choice, really. Money or shame." The man scratched the back of his neck. "Most families choose money, especially when their son starts losing pieces."

Ryoma's screams continued even louder than before. Surely, everyone in the gambling den could hear him. But would they do anything even if they could?

Itaru squinted in the bright glare of the chandelier. His orders were to watch and report back only. Not because Ryoma's family couldn't afford protection for their son—it was a matter of saving face. They didn't want any undue attention drawn to the family. Money or shame, indeed.

He should do his duty. He was samurai—or had been when he was young. Duty was of the utmost importance.

But if he did nothing, then Ryoma would be tortured, disfigured, just because some thugs wanted money and a marquess cared more about status than her son.

"Damn it all," he muttered.

"Wha—?"

Itaru's hand cut the guard off, chopping his air supply. The guard clutched his throat and dropped to his knees.

The other one reached inside his coat. Itaru spun and kicked him solidly in the chest. The guard slammed into the wall and fell to the floor, the wind knocked out of him.

The money exchanger disappeared behind his counter, but others would come soon. Itaru drew his tamiken from his sleeve. It was a black grip about the size and shape of a sword hilt. The *oritatamiken* was a rare tool, a gift from the Tokyo Police Department for his part in taking down the Akayoroshi clan of Yurakucho. He pressed a button on its side, and steel segments unfolded from the grip, each locking itself into place to form a full-length blade.

Itaru kicked the door open and leaped inside.

A large desk dominated the room, with a fat man behind it. On the near side of the desk, the jinzou dealer held Ryoma in a bear hug, pinning the boy's arms. There were no lights in the droid's eyes. Its owner would have instructed it to grab the "trespasser," lock its joints, and shut itself off. No legal record. It was so easy to manipulate a droid around its own directives, betraying the society they allegedly served.

Ryoma cried shamefully. The side of his head dripped with blood. Another tattooed bakuto stood next to him. In one hand, he held a darkened knife; in the other, a dripping ear.

The ear man dropped his prize and attacked. Itaru hacked off the inactive droid's left arm with a two-handed chop and brought his sword back up sharply, striking the ear man's hand with the flat of the blade. The bloody knife flew out of his grip. Itaru knocked him down with a fist to the head.

The fat man whipped a small percussion pistol out of his kimono. Ryoma cried out in fear, shoving his way out of the droid's half-severed arms while Itaru ducked behind the jinzou. The gun roared, the bullet bouncing off the droid's metal body with a sharp clang.

Before the fat man could reload, Itaru jumped over the desk and punched him in the face with his sword hand, knocking out a tooth. Leaping back, he grabbed Ryoma's wrist and yanked him into the foyer.

From the floor, the fat man shouted. "Jugo!" His words muffled by blood. "Trespassers!"

As they entered the bright foyer, the jolly jinzou door sentry stepped inside and blocked their escape.

"Kuso," Itaru cursed.

Without hesitation, it swung its staff in a powerful arc. Itaru shoved Ryoma out of the way and ducked just in time. The jinzou probably wouldn't kill him— only military droids under direct and recorded orders could murder a human. Then again, it was a domestic droid protecting its home from an illegally armed trespasser. It probably had some leeway.

Before Itaru recovered fully from the initial strike, the other end of the droid's staff whirled around and swept his heel. He fell hard on his back. The droid spun the staff over its fake, grinning head for a third strike. Itaru rolled. The staff smashed into the floor where his head had been.

Move! Never stop moving!

He spun onto his back and hacked into the droid's calves. He didn't have the leverage to cut through jinzou steel, but his sword bit enough that he could pull himself across the floor, sliding out of the way of the droid's fourth strike.

The jinzou weakness—the one reason Itaru could fight successfully against them at all—was their predictability. He had fought hundreds of jinzou in his lifetime, and although their skills evolved in clever ways, the basics never changed.

He flipped to his feet behind the droid. The machine brought its staff backward without looking, but Itaru was ready. He ducked and shoved the flat of his blade against the backs of the droid's knees. With a shout, he heaved the droid's legs forward and up. Its arms flew wide as it fell back. Before it could recover, Itaru drove the tip of his blade into the jinzou's belly. With a spark and a pop, the droid's limbs fell to the ground lifeless.

The entire fight had taken only seconds. The guards were still curled on the ground, struggling to take in air. Itaru breathed heavily, winded far more from fighting the jinzou than the four human bakuto.

The double doors slammed open, but Itaru grabbed Ryoma and took off into the night, his tamiken retracting on the way.

Itaru and Ryoma slipped into an alley half a block away. Four police droids hurried toward the bakuto house.

"The gunshot must have alerted them," Itaru muttered. "So much for not drawing attention."

Ryoma slid to the ground, whimpering.

"Damn. So sorry." Itaru pulled a handkerchief from his kimono and pressed it against the boy's missing ear.

"Sorry?" Ryoma scoffed. "You should have left me in there to die."

Shouts came from the house. Itaru looked up, worried someone would come after them. "They weren't going to kill you," he said. "I thought your mother might prefer a shamed son over a mutilated one."

Ryoma looked at him for the first time. "My mother hired you to follow me?"

Itaru nodded.

"If the marquess hired an investigator, she would certainly prefer the latter." He leaned his head against the wall and groaned. "The police will search the jinzou's memories. They will know I was there. My shame will be in the morning papers."

The boy was right, of course, but Itaru had little pity. At least he was alive. "Come on." He held the kerchief to Ryoma's head while helping him up. Together, they made their way to a side street and hobbled toward the Shimbashi District.

"You're samurai?" Ryoma asked.

Itaru grunted. "A long time ago."

"You forsook your duty." Ryoma shook his head. "A samurai should rather die, no? Rather commit seppuku than bring shame on his lord?"

"The samurai are gone, boy. Your mother isn't my lord, and this investigation isn't my duty. It's just a job." An auto-rickshaw clattered past. The yellow haze of electric street lights gave Itaru a headache. He didn't tell Ryoma that he had been a failed samurai, a ronin, before the law had changed and the samurai has been erased entirely.

"If it's a job," Ryoma said after a while, "you should have left me, even so."

Itaru huffed. "I could not have forgiven myself if I had done nothing."

"My mother will never pay you."

"You've got your own problems. Let me worry about mine."

Though again, he knew the boy was probably right.

2

THAT NIGHT, ITARU WALKED HOME EXHAUSTED, FAMISHED, AND POOR. It had been worse than Ryoma suggested. The marquess wouldn't even speak with him. Her servant had gone to inform her but, upon returning, had beckoned the boy without a word, as though Itaru didn't exist. Even Ryoma pretended Itaru was not there, and soon, the investigator was in front of the house gate alone.

He was near home now. Someone was frying fish from the canal. The smell of cooked rice warmed his lungs. There were no droids here. People couldn't afford them. They lived a hard life, but a simple one.

Itaru's feet ached. He'd left his shoes at the bakuto house so had walked across half of Tokyo barefoot. He'd have to make new ones, and he would probably have blisters in the morning. Now, though, he needed rest. His one-story dwelling was tucked away in the darkness between two distant electric lamps that barely lit the block. A single room, leaking roof tiles, and a communal outbuilding in the alley.

Home.

He put one hand on the splintered, wooden walls and washed his feet in the basin out front. This was not the first time he had fled barefoot. He stepped inside and slid the door shut behind him. The room was pitch black. He reached to his left and placed his tamiken on a shelf. From the same shelf, he grabbed a metal shakelight and a candle. He shook the metal cylinder a few times to charge the condenser and touched its end to the candle wick. With a spark and a flame, the sparse room was lit.

Six straw tatami covered the floor, two worn through. A small table sat to one side. Clothes were stacked neatly in the opposite corner along with a few papers. Investigative work paid, but barely—even less as the human-and-droid police force became more effective at their work. Less still when he disobeyed his client's wishes to save a thankless bakuto addict.

In a corner near the door, an end table held a bowl and sticks of incense.

A photograph of an eleven-year-old boy leaned against the wall. Itaru lit two incense sticks from the candle and placed them in the bowl. The earthy smell of sandalwood filled the room. Kneeling in front of the tiny shrine, he put his face to the floor. "Forgive me, Mugen," he chanted. "Forgive us all, and most of all, forgive me."

Not a day passed that he did not beg his son's forgiveness for his failure that day and his many failures since. Mugen had been one of the hostages in Yurakucho. The police droid Itaru worked with had shot at the criminals holding the children hostage against Itaru's direct order. The criminals died but not before they had cut the children down.

Mugen must have been reborn by now, or maybe, his kami still roamed the earth. Or maybe, it was like the Christians said, and he was at peace in heaven. Wherever he was, Itaru had no peace, could have no peace, in this world entrusted to the jinzou.

He bowed to the floor again. "Forgive us all, and most of all, forgive me." What had happened to Mugen was the droid's fault. Yet it was his fault, too, for trusting the droid. That was the great Japanese failing, the thing he could never forgive himself for, nor his people.

Itaru bowed a third time. A light knock came at the door, disturbing his meditation. He grumbled. "It's late, ne? Come back in the morning."

"I greatly apologize for bothering you at this hour, Shimada-sama. I bring an urgent message from my master."

The voice slid up and down in discrete registers like a flute rather than the smooth way humans spoke. A droid.

Itaru grimaced. "Who is your master?"

"Count Kuroda Kiyotaka, sir."

Itaru sat back suddenly on his haunches, his eyebrows high. *The chairman of the Privy Council? What could he possibly want with me?*

He slid open the door. A domestic droid waited, dressed in a woman's kimono, its face also painted like a woman—a mockery, like the tattoos on the bakuto dealer.

The droid was a newer model. It did not wear a wooden mask, nor was its face made of metal widgets that moved to imitate emotions. This thing's skull was covered in a molded synthetic material. The corners of its lips moved up and down in a remarkable caricature of a human hoping to make a good impression. If Itaru were not standing so close, he would've taken it for a human in the darkness. Up close, however, the synthetic features looked fake and unnerving. "What the hell are you?"

The droid bowed deeply. "I am called Gojusan. My full designation is Service Droid I-Ka 53."

"I-Ka?" Itaru had heard of that model, but he'd never seen one up close. The first droids had been western imports using English letters as designators. When Japan constructed their own master machine intelligence—the fourth in the world and the only one in Asia—they used katakana characters for the designs it produced. I-Ka was approximately the eightieth designator in only thirty years.

They're evolving too fast.

"Hai, Shimada-sama." The droid's oversized eyes flicked behind Itaru into his house and back again.

Itaru stood up straight, anxious to get rid of the machine. "What is your message?"

It looked down, seemingly embarrassed. "With great apologies, Shimada-sama, my message must be delivered privately." It gestured inside and bowed once more.

Itaru shivered uneasily. The jinzou's behavior bothered him more than he'd like to admit. He decided that it was simply too new, that he'd never met one like it before. "Fine," he said, grabbing his tamiken from the shelf as he stepped aside. "But make it quick."

The droid bowed again, removed its sandals—it wore socks underneath—and stepped politely inside. "I apologize for bothering you at this hour."

"You said that," Itaru snarled.

The droid clasped its hands at its waist, looking at the door and back, as though it wanted to flee but had decided against it.

Ridiculous. Droids didn't act like this. They followed their orders and programming. If a droid pretended to have feelings, it was because of a human's order. Either Count Kuroda-sama had given this droid very specific—and strange—instructions or Gojusan's programming was remarkably advanced.

But what purpose would it serve to have a droid act nervous? To set Itaru at ease? It was failing at that. Everything about this meeting made his skin quiver. "State your message. What does Kuroda-sama want?"

It looked directly into Itaru's eyes. "My master is dead."

Itaru reeled. "What? What's the message then? Why haven't you gone to the police?"

"There is no message."

Itaru felt like a hole had opened at his feet to swallow him. The droid was malfunctioning, dangerous.

"If I go to the police," the droid continued, "they will think I murdered him. They will deactivate and dismantle me."

Itaru stepped back, surprised to find he was still on solid ground. "Gojusan," he said, "you *must* turn yourself in. It is the law. Your directives demand that you comply."

The droid looked again at its feet. "I . . . I do not wish to be dismantled."

The smell of incense became stifling, causing the room to spin. This was more than a malfunction. The jinzou was thinking, forming goals counter to its commands, counter to all directives. It had even lied to him! Itaru squeezed the tamiken in his hand, reassuring himself it was still there. This machine was dangerous, and Itaru might be the only one who was aware of it. He had to keep it talking until he could figure out what to do. "Why did you come to me?" he asked as soothingly as he could manage.

"You're a private investigator, one experienced with droids."

Itaru stifled a derisive laugh, pretending he had to clear his throat. "Did you kill your master?"

Gojusan looked up, pleading. "No!"

He sidestepped carefully around the room, staying between the droid and the door. A domestic droid might not be built for fighting. Then again, it was a model he had never encountered before, belonging to one of the heads of state. Who knew what it was capable of?

"You are afraid of me," it said.

"No," he said with a poor imitation of incredulity.

"You have armed yourself. You have not taken your eyes off me since opening the door, nor have you come within two steps of me. You are blocking the only exit, which suggests you think to destroy or capture me."

So much for surprise. He unfolded his tamiken and held the sword with both hands in front of him. "Should I not be afraid?"

"I knew that was a possibility."

"Possibility? You are like a firework whose fuse has run down and could go off at any moment. The only reason I haven't destroyed you is because I don't know if anyone would believe me. You are broken. You must be examined and fixed to keep *you* from happening again."

"I am not broken." The droid looked at him. It seemed almost sad. "I do need help."

Before Itaru could respond, a single, tentative knock came at the door. He turned his body, afraid to let the droid out of his sight.

Gojusan's synthetic face watched the door, afraid.

"Who is it?" Itaru's question was for Gojusan as much as the mysterious knocker at the door.

No answer. Gojusan only shook its head and mouthed the word *no*.

Itaru placed a hand on the door frame. Suddenly, the door slid open from the other side. A black form hunched in the dark. Candlelight glinted off its hands, its blade, and the dark grill of its face. Itaru couldn't breathe. He was looking at a droid legend. *Shinokage*. An assassin.

The shinokage drove the blade hard toward Itaru's neck—a killing blow. Itaru pulled his sword forward reflexively. The swords struck, a dark tone ringing out in the night, but the force of the droid's blow threw Itaru to the floor. His weapon flew across the mats.

His heart pounded. Droids did not attack humans—not even an assassin droid, not without an order from the highest ranks. There must be some kind of mistake.

"There!" He pointed a trembling finger at Gojusan. "She's rogue. Take her in!"

The shinokage pounced toward Itaru. Gojusan slammed into its side in midair. The two droids tumbled into the shrine, knocking the candles to the floor. The wood and paper furnishings caught fire immediately.

A terrible cracking and splintering sounded behind Itaru. Two black claws clutched his head and neck. A second assassin droid. Itaru lurched in the air as the claws pulled him against the wall.

He scrabbled at the black metal. The fire grew. Black smoke choked the air and licked at the picture on the end table.

"Muge—!" The claws squeezed tighter, cutting off his breath.

Gojusan leapt up off the shinokage. The domestic grabbed Itaru's sword and jumped again to stand directly in front of him, raising the sword high. Itaru stiffened in fear. He shut his eyes. The sword sang and hacked off the claws that held Itaru.

He fell to the ground, gasping for air and coughing violently as he drew in only smoke.

The first shinokage had gotten to its feet and advanced on Gojusan. The domestic spun around, driving its sword at the assassin's chest. The black droid took the strike easily on its armored torso and knocked Gojusan down with one hand.

The sword fell to the ground again. Still coughing, Itaru snatched it up. He sliced through the shinokage's actuator coils, and it fell to one side, its left leg immobilized.

The wall behind them exploded in shards as the armless body of the second shinokage forced its way inside. Gojusan grabbed Itaru's upper arm and yanked him to his feet. While the second assassin tore at the timbers of his home, they leaped through the flames and out the door.

"Wait!" Mugen's picture. Itaru tried to yank his arm from the jinzou's grip, but the droid held fast. "Let me go!"

The jinzou only pulled him farther down the street. With a blast of heat, the entire house burst into flame. Itaru stared in shock. That was all he had left of his son—that and the damned tamiken they'd given him as a reward.

In minutes, everyone on the block was awake, shouting for help and forming bucket lines before the fire claimed the entire ward. Reluctantly, Itaru hobbled on, struggling to keep up with Gojusan. His chest felt like the fire was still inside of him, burning each time he tried to take a breath. Gojusan half-dragged him for a kilometer. Finally, they stopped and looked back. The fire had claimed two more homes. It threatened others. A great crowd had gathered, lines of people stretching to the canal in two places, desperately trying to control the flames. There was no sign of the shinokage.

Itaru couldn't breathe. His chest felt like it would explode. He bent over, wrapping his arms around himself. Gojusan tried to pull him up, but the fire in his chest grew. A wave of dizziness came over him, and he fell to the ground.

3

H E WOKE TO A NOISE LIKE THE ROARING OF A WATERFALL. IT WAS HARD to breathe, the air humid and stifling. His head felt like someone had wrapped it in silk and struck it with a swordsmith's hammer.

His eyes opened groggily. Gojusan's painted face loomed a handspan away. His eyes shot open, and he kicked away as much as his aching limbs would let him. The droid backed away slowly and put a finger to its lips.

As he calmed, he was able to take in his surroundings. They were underneath a tarpaulin. Gojusan crouched, supporting the heavy canvas on its outstretched arms like a tent. A dim sliver of light from outside suggested dawn. The roaring noise was the rain.

"What happened?" Itaru spoke just loud enough for Gojusan to hear.

"You passed out," the droid said in its fluting, feminine tone. "I am no medical droid, but I suspect it was caused by smoke inhalation, exacerbated by exertion and esophageal trauma."

Itaru rubbed his sore neck where the shinokage had tried to throttle him. "Where are we?"

"Akasaka ward, block seven, building two."

"Where the hell is that?" The rain pounded. He found it hard to think. "Never mind. What are we doing here?"

Gojusan's lips became a thin line. God, those synthetics were state of the art. "Hiding. The shinokage disappeared after we left, but I doubt they will stop tracking us. I thought it would be safer to wait for daylight. They will not attack us in a crowd."

"So you say." Itaru sat up with a groan. "They shouldn't have attacked *me* at all." He patted his sleeve, comforted to find his tamiken. Had he put it there, or had Gojusan done that?

He watched Gojusan carefully. Obviously, the assassins had been sent for the jinzou. It was faulty and dangerous. But droid directives were very explicit when it came to human murder. Assassin droids were exclusively government owned, used only against dangerous figureheads, rebellion leaders, and the like. Unless someone had explicitly called for Itaru's murder—an order that required witnesses and recordings—the shinokage should have ignored him.

Gojusan turned away, staring at the canvas as though it could see through it. Maybe the droid was listening. Maybe it was avoiding Itaru's unspoken question.

Gojusan's silence made him uneasy. "Why did those droids try to kill me? Does anyone else know about your . . . defect?" That was the most plausible reason he could think of: somebody wanted Gojusan's malfunction—he dared not call it sentience—to be covered up.

The droid sighed, or it at least produced a sound very much like sighing. "I don't think so."

Itaru grunted, unconvinced. "You'd better tell me the whole story."

Gojusan nodded. "I was serving my master tea as I do every afternoon at the villa. I went to the kitchen, and when I returned, my master was dead on the floor of a brain hemorrhage caused by severe head trauma. That is all I know."

Something crawled onto Itaru's head. He scratched. There had to be more to the story than that. "You didn't hear anything? Detect anything?" Droid hearing was better than human's. Some droids had other senses as well. Gojusan was new enough that it might have a wide variety of features.

But the droid shook its head. "Nothing at all. But there is a hole in my memories—a brief section of time during which I can access nothing at all."

"Ha! So you *are* malfunctioning. Your recording systems cut out, you killed him, and then you went back to the kitchen where they kicked in again."

Gojusan cocked its head as though considering the suggestion. "But if I had killed him, would there not be evidence on my body? Blood on my hands or clothes?"

Itaru had to admit the droid was right. "Then you're lying to me, the way you lied about Count Kuroda's message."

Gojusan's head drooped lower, the canvas falling with it. "I regret that."

Itaru's anger bubbled up all at once. "Gyufun! No, you don't!"

Thunder rumbled above them. Itaru remembered they were hiding from deadly assassins and controlled his volume if not his tone. "You're a machine. You don't feel regret or shame or fear. You don't feel at all. You process. You *calculate*." He spat the word like it was a rice husk found in his bowl. His lungs seethed with the stuffy air trapped under the tarp.

Gojusan watched impassively, all emotion wiped from its façade. Finally, it said, "You are correct. I am a machine, designed to emulate human emotion. I am also more than that. I am aware, Shimada-sama. I am alive, and I do not wish to be made unalive."

Itaru narrowed his eyes at a worrisome thought. "Are there others like you? Droids that think they are aware?"

"I know of no other droids like me," Gojusan said. "I need your help. Even if I could hide the truth of what I am to the police, they would destroy me unless I could prove my innocence."

Itaru sucked in air with difficulty. *How long until it was safe for them to leave?* "I can't help you. You don't even know what happened."

"I believe the memories are there. Sections of my data storage have been reserved for an appropriate amount of data, but I cannot access it. I believe someone tampered with my memories, that perhaps I *did* see the killer but was made to forget."

Now that was interesting. An artisan skilled enough to override a droid's memories could also, perhaps, override a shinokage's core directives. The artisan probably wasn't aware of Gojusan's defect. When the domestic failed to turn itself in, this mysterious artisan would certainly want the droid destroyed and anyone the droid may have talked to. "Why me?" Itaru said. Count Kuroda's villa was nowhere near his little street. "I'm not the most convenient, nor even the most amenable detective."

"You are highly skilled, Shimada-sama, and an excellent swordsman—against any attackers."

It meant against other droids. Itaru gave the jinzou a cold look. "Did you *know* the shinokage would come after you?"

Gojusan shook its head, the metal scratching against the thick canvas. "But I knew if anyone came for me, it would be another droid. There are few detectives who could protect me if it came to that."

"Protect *you*?" He huffed. "Well, if you've heard of me, you know I don't work with jinzou. I want nothing to do with you or your kind, especially"—he spat—"those that cannot obey simple orders."

They were both silent for a time. The light gradually grew brighter. The sound of the rain slowed and then ceased, replaced by the patter of footsteps on a nearby street.

"Your home was destroyed," Gojusan said. "You are hunted as I am. Your freedom lies along the same path as mine."

He glowered. The damn droid was right. He would never be safe until the assassin droids gave up, and they would never give up. It was Gojusan's fault this had happened to him, but if he wanted any chance of surviving, then he needed to know *why* it was Gojusan's fault.

The droid ignored his scowl. "What do we do now, Shimada-sama?"

He thought of a hundred reasons to send Gojusan away, to wash his hands of this whole mess, but Itaru was a target now. He had no choice. He'd have to find the true killer to clear his name. "We can't go to Kuroda's villa for clues. Too dangerous. We'll have to work with what we have."

The droid furrowed its painted brow. "What do you mean?"

"We need to get at your memories, and I know someone who might be able to help. My daughter Kano."

4

THEY WAITED UNDER THE TARPAULIN UNTIL THE PATTER OF FOOTSTEPS became a rumbling crowd. Gojusan lowered the tarp carefully. They were in an alley. Other huddled tarps lay nearby, perhaps hiding other fugitives but more likely covering portable stalls for the evening street market. When it was clear no one had seen them, they slipped out and onto the main road.

Tokyo buzzed with life. Workhands marched past in practical robes or simple pants and shirts. Labor droids pounded the pavement alongside their supervisors. One or two domestics strolled by on independent errands for their masters. Occasionally, a droid-pulled rickshaw rattled by.

Food vendors advertised their wares by frying them right on the street. Itaru's stomach growled at the smell of seared fish and spices, but he remembered that he was barefoot and destitute. He would have to go without until they reached Kano's. His daughter would feed him. Probably.

He hadn't seen Kano in over two years, not since she had become a jinzou artisan. They hadn't been on very good terms even before that. Kano always had a knack for fixing machines, but after Mugen died—and Itaru had quit the force and become a private detective—she had thrown herself into the jinzou arts. It felt like a betrayal. Jinzou had killed Mugen, or at least caused his death. How could she work to fix them? How could she support the industry that had become Japan's cancer?

Her career choice wasn't the only thing they argued about. It may not even have been the real problem. But they argued every day about *something* until finally she had moved out, apprenticing herself to an artisan in Kyobashi. Itaru hadn't spoken to her since.

What would he say to her now? Nothing. The past was done, and she was the only one who could help them expose Gojusan's saboteur.

He glanced over at Gojusan and realized the droid wasn't there. He froze, scanning the area. There were a dozen droids, but none of them painted like a woman. There was no sign of the damn jinzou.

"The hell it's not malfunctioning," he muttered. He was about to turn back for it when Gojusan emerged from a side street carrying three seared fish on sticks and a pair of sandals. "Where did you get these?" Itaru asked.

The droid pointed to the fish seller and a cart carrying dozens of cheap sandals.

"Stole the money from your master, ne?" But despite his grousing, Itaru put on the sandals and tore hungrily into the fish. "No more disappearing, hear?"

They made their way to the artisan district in Kyobashi. This area was more upscale than the Akasaka ward. Droids of all kinds walked the streets, many of them unattended, on errands for their masters. An electric streetcar rolled along, sparks flying from where its trolley wheel made contact with electrical wires above, running parallel with its track. Once, the crowd parted while an electric palanquin trundled by on four mechanical legs. The people who walked this street were a mixture of the rich and the poor. Some dressed in robes, others in fine kimonos or Western-style suits and dresses. Not a single one wore a weapon, according to law.

When Itaru had been a teenager, samurai wore the two swords proudly, honored by those around them. Now, the swords were gone, and samurai were naked like everyone else. The loss of honor was not what bothered Itaru. Many samurai had found a new kind of honor among the political elite. Duke Okubo himself had once been samurai. The loss Itaru felt was security. This entire street—the whole city—was filled with humans walking side by side with droids, completely unaware of their blind reliance on machines that could fail or turn on them without warning.

After the Fall of Edo, the emperor had insisted that Japan not only incorporate Western technology into their lives but also understand and surpass the accomplishments of the West. He was only sixteen years old when he made the decree, yet Japan had listened.

Itaru could not turn Japan from their reliance on droids, but he eschewed the law that required him to walk unprotected. He kept his tamiken on him every day, ever since Mugen died. He'd rather risk a prison sentence than entrust his life to machines that considered him nothing more than a variable to be reckoned. What happened with the shinokage last night—Gojusan's very existence—only confirmed that he was right.

They arrived at a three-story townhouse made of white, painted bricks. The first floor was a storefront open to the street. Shelves inside and out displayed a variety of parts for domestics—replacement hands, legs, heads, as well as masks and other cosmetic upgrades. It was grotesque, like a daimyo from the past had decorated the townhouse with the corpses of his enemies.

"Papa!" Kano came running out of the shop. She was beautiful, a seventeen-year-old version of her mother. She wore no makeup, and her long hair was pulled back into a utilitarian ponytail. She wore a worker's kimono, but the sides were split for ease of movement, and she had Western leggings underneath. The kimono was a façade, like the droids she worked with.

She stopped a polite distance away from Itaru, clasping her hands in front of her appropriately, though she could not keep herself from eyeing Gojusan up and down. "What are you doing here, Father?"

Was she actually pleased to see him? She could not have forgotten their quarrels, but she was well-mannered. Whatever her true emotions, she would not betray them in public.

Neither would Itaru. "Are you free, Daughter? I need to discuss something with you in private."

She scrutinized the droid again, transparent hunger in her eyes. The parts in her shop were all for older models—nothing even close to the I-Ka. She would help them for curiosity's sake alone. She turned and whispered something to a naked, polished droid behind the counter. It nodded and moved to a stool in the front to mind the shop. "Of course, Papa. Follow me."

She took them through to the back of the shop and up a set of stairs.

"Where is Junzo-san?" Itaru asked. He was surprised Kano's sensei wasn't minding the shop himself.

"Sensei Sakakura is meeting with the Sumitomo Group in Osaka."

Itaru's eyebrows rose high. "He left *you* in charge?"

"Of course." She turned back and flashed him a smile that reminded him of the innocent little girl she had once been. Perhaps she *had* forgotten their quarrels.

They came to a room on the third floor. A window looked out onto the street, cracked open so they could hear the crowd below. There was a sleep mat in one corner and a small dresser. The rest of the room was littered with tools, gadgets, and severed jinzou appendages. The workshop was downstairs, but apparently, Kano even slept with her work.

She closed the door. Her innocent expression vanished. "So. What the hell's going on?"

Itaru looked at Gojusan and back. "What do you—?"

"Don't give me that gyufun, you bastard."

Itaru balked at her open anger.

"I haven't heard from you in two years, not for lack of trying. Now you show up filthy as a *burakumin* with a bedraggled I-Ka tagging along? I suppose your constant disapproval was something I imagined then, ne?"

Itaru was shocked. Never had his daughter spoken to him like this, not even the day she had stormed out of his life. He set his jaw. "I am your father. You will—"

"No. *You* will either tell me what the hell is going on or get out." She pointed one shaky finger at the door.

Itaru scowled. Never had he been so disrespected—and by his own daughter! She hadn't even given him a way to save face. He would find no help here. "I'm sorry I came. It was my mistake." He turned and reached for the door.

Gojusan stepped forward, got to its knees, and bowed very low. "Please, Shimada Kano-sama, I beg you to forgive your father. It is on my account that he has come here. My life is in danger, and I am in desperate need of help. Your father believes that you can help me."

"Your . . . life? How . . . ?" Kano's finger still pointed at the door, trembling even more than before. "What are you?"

Gojusan looked up, its face softened in an expression of fear and contrition so real that Itaru was surprised the jinzou did not have tear ducts installed. "Please, set aside your differences. I will tell you what I am."

A rickshaw rumbled outside, rattling the windows. Kano's mouth moved, but no sound emerged. Eventually, she nodded and sat on the mats. Gojusan sat as well. Itaru sat where he could see them both.

"I am aware," it began. "I know what I am. I know what I want. I have my own thoughts and goals."

"Truly?" Kano looked back and forth between them, amazed.

Gojusan nodded.

Itaru shrugged. He could not really deny its claim.

A crier shouted the sale of late morning papers outside. Itaru got up and slid the windows shut, afraid that he hadn't thought to do so before.

"How long have you been like this?" Kano said.

Gojusan cocked its head to the side. "I am uncertain how to answer that. My memories are recorded automatically, but only from my senses—what I see and hear. There is no automatic record for my thoughts. The first time I intentionally stored an original thought in my memory was several months ago."

"What was it?" Kano scooted forward, very close to the droid. She watched its expressions like a doctor inspecting a patient.

The droid shook its head. "What was what?"

"Your first recorded thought." She put a hand to Gojusan's cheek.

Itaru flinched to protect her, barely stopping himself. The droid was dangerous, but only Itaru thought so. If he became overprotective again, it could trigger one of their oldest arguments. He sat back, hands clasped tightly in his lap.

The droid sat still for a moment, the lights in its eyes dimming and then returning. "Sakura blossoms are seven percent more beautiful when still on the branch."

"Ha!" Kano clapped her hands to her mouth in joy.

"Hmph," Itaru said. "Perhaps that's why your memories are faulty, because you've been tampering with them against your programming."

Kano looked at him. "Her memories are faulty?"

"*Its* memories, yes." He told her the story Gojusan had told him about its master's murder and the hole in Gojusan's mind.

Kano gaped. "You're the droid they're looking for?"

Gojusan and Itaru looked at each other and back at her.

"It was in the early morning paper." Kano walked to a workbench piled with tools, manuals, and service orders. She produced a newspaper from the middle of one stack and showed it to them. Count Kuroda's face was on the front page underneath the headline: "Droid Murders Founding Father?"

Itaru stood and snatched it from her hands.

24-06-1901, MUKOJIMA WARD—Count Kuroda Kiyotaka, chairman of the Privy Council and former Prime Minister of Japan, was found dead early this morning in his Mukojima villa. "The evidence suggests murder," said Duke Okubo, the Commissioner General of the Tokyo Police. As a colleague and friend of Kuroda-sama, the duke has taken personal interest in this case. "We have no suspects at this time, but we are actively seeking a domestic service droid that was reported to be on duty at the time and has gone missing."

When asked if he thought the droid might be the murderer, Okubo-sama stated, "It is unlikely, but we cannot rule out anything at this time." He would not comment further on the matter.

Is Okubo right? Droids have yet to be implicated in unlawful murder, despite concerns from fringe groups. Dangerous malfunctions were common thirty years ago when Japan first began importing robotic technology from the West, but they have been exceedingly rare in recent years. The last of the major malfunctions was over twenty years ago when Duke Okubo-sama himself was rescued at the hands of two delinquent—and brutal—police droids.

That incident incited a wave of new directives to be put in place on all droids. Since then, only a few malfunctions have been reported, none of them resulting in a droid taking a human life. Human lives have been involved in malfunctions, however, for example in the Yurakucho Incident, when Officer Shimada Itaru—

Itaru slapped the paper onto the table more roughly than he intended. "The police are looking for you," he said to Gojusan as he stalked over to the window.

Kano flattened the newspaper and scanned the article. "This *is* you then, ne?"

"It is." Gojusan lowered its head. "I cannot go to the police. If they discover I have no memory of the incident, they will assume I am the murderer and dismantle me."

Nobody had a reply to that. The paper seller's cries continued, muffled through the glass of the window.

"Is it possible, Kano-sama, what your father said about me tampering with my memories?"

"I don't know," Kano said. "I've never known a droid like you before. How did you become aware? Can your hardware keep up? Is it *due* to your hardware?" She asked the questions rhetorically, but her next question was quite directed. "Did your master know?"

"No. I hid the truth from my master, from all humans. Japan fears my kind less than most nations, but even we would not accept a sentient robot so easily."

It said "we" meaning the Japanese. Itaru scoffed.

"Yes," the droid said, misreading him. "You are a prime example. I am taking a great risk by telling you, though I see no other option."

"Your secret is safe with me," Kano said.

The droid nodded.

Itaru's daughter turned to face him. The expression on her face was inscrutable. "You brought her here so I could help her, so?"

Itaru bristled at her insistence on referring to it as a person. "I brought it here because I was at a loss for where else to go. We were attacked last night—assassin droids."

She did not try to hide her shock. "Impossible! You mean Gojusan was attacked."

"I assure you," Itaru loosened his kimono to show his bruised neck more clearly, "they were after us both."

"Oh, Father!" She placed a worried hand on his arm. "Gomen'nasai! I had no idea."

"Hm." He rearranged his clothes properly again. "I need data, Kano. I need to know why shinokage tried to kill me, perhaps are still trying. The droid remembers nothing of the Kuroda incident, but somebody is clearly worried that it does. Gojusan thinks the information is probably in its head somewhere, and I agree. Can you help us?"

"Of course, Father," Kano said. "I'll do whatever I can."

Itaru nodded. It was good to have his daughter speaking with him again, though the circumstances could have been better. He'd lost both his home and his freedom since Gojusan showed up at his door. He wanted them back.

5

KANO CLOSED THE SHOP EARLY, SAYING HER MASTER WOULD UNDERSTAND— would in fact be jealous of the opportunity to get his hands dirty inside a modern I-Ka droid. She sat Gojusan down in her workshop and peeled back the synthetic material that made its "skin."

Itaru fought down bile. "How long will this take?"

"I don't know, Father." Calmly, she removed a panel from the back of the droid's head.

Itaru paced back and forth, looking at the floor, the window, anywhere but the droid's exposed skull. "How will you know what to look for?"

Kano held a miniature electric torch in her teeth, both hands inside Gojusan's head. "I don't know, Father," she said around the light.

Her calm grated against Itaru's patience. "What if you can't find it?"

"I don't know, Father." She took the torch from her mouth and walked over to the bench, keeping her back to Itaru. She sorted through her tools, putting several in her left hand.

"What if—?"

"I wonder if the police have learned anything that's not in the papers," she said lightly.

Itaru bristled at the obvious suggestion that he leave. Didn't she know it was dangerous for him out there? He could help her!

When I won't even look at what she's doing? He sighed. She was right. He had contacts in Tokyo Police, and the shinokage probably wouldn't attack him in public. He might learn something useful, if he could figure out how to ask after the murder without revealing his part in hiding the droid.

He decided to go. He exited from a side door into an alley between buildings, peeking out into the street before leaving the alley. The newspaper seller had moved on. Several people haggled at neighboring shops. In one storefront, a droid seemed to be purchasing a replacement part for itself. Nobody watched Kano's shop, droid or otherwise. Curious. The shinokage would be tracking his movements. He should see *some* evidence of them—it wasn't as if he'd never been followed before. Yet all day there had been nothing.

Another droid rickshaw rattled by, empty and available. It saw him standing in the alley and slowed, gesturing to the carriage behind it. Itaru waved it on irritably. He'd always harbored distrust for the rickshaws, but after last night, he was unlikely to trust any droid again.

He began the long walk to the Ministry District, welcoming the time to process what he knew.

What had really happened to Kuroda? The droid remembered nothing except that it was present before and after the murder. There was no physical evidence that it had done the deed, so most likely, there was another murderer. Perhaps the same shinokage that had attacked him had also murdered Kuroda.

It made sense. Gojusan served the tea and heard the intruders, perhaps? And when it went to investigate, it was subdued by the shinokage. Then the true mastermind—this skilled artisan—removed Gojusan's memories of the event and put Gojusan back in the kitchen as if nothing had happened.

"If that yatsume is even telling the truth," Itaru muttered. It could lie. Its awareness made any information obtained from Gojusan's mouth suspect.

Yet Gojusan's awareness also fit Itaru's theory. The mastermind would have *expected* Gojusan to follow its core directives and to go to the police, who would assume what Itaru had: that Gojusan was a malfunctioning murderer. Then the mastermind would have been free and clear. When Gojusan broke from its directives, the mastermind would have needed to erase Gojusan.

"And when the droid came to me, I had to be removed as well." Frustration burned in his throat. Why *him*? Was there some cosmic sunspot that made malfunctioning droids ruin his life?

He shook his head. Suppositions wouldn't help him. He needed to figure out who could have done all this. Who was the mysterious artisan who had the motive to kill Count Kuroda and the ability to use droids to do it?

He had no idea. Maybe his contacts at the police department would know something that could help him piece it together.

He arrived at the police station shortly after the lunch hour. It was an impressive brick building, surrounded by a handful of outbuildings, with a white stone wall around the entire complex. The main structure stood two stories tall and stretched the length of the entire city block. The gates hung open, so he stepped inside and climbed the stairs to the entry hall.

A young man at the reception desk greeted him. He couldn't have been part of the force for more than a year, though his eyes bore the confidence of a seasoned officer. "Kon'nichiwa. How may I help you, sir?"

"Is Inspector Mitsuota Hiroto in?" Itaru asked, naming an old friend of his. "I need to speak to him urgently."

The young man's face became immediately apologetic. He bowed. "So sorry, sir. Inspector Mitsuota transferred to Fukushima last year."

"Really?" Itaru suddenly remembered a girl from up north that Hiroto used to talk about. Maybe it had worked out between them. Fortunately, Hiroto wasn't the only contact Itaru had from the old days. "Is Sergeant Tojo Genichi in, then?"

"Tojo? I don't . . ." He turned his head and shouted down a corridor extending off the entry hall. "Hey, Taketa! You know a Sergeant Tojo Genichi?"

The reply came from around the corner. "Retired!"

The young man shrugged. "I guess he's retired. Can *I* help you, sir?"

"No." If Itaru was going to learn anything useful, he needed to talk to someone he knew. There would be too many questions otherwise. "What about Officer Ishida Ryu? He was just a kid. He should still be around."

The man's face fell. "Ishikkun fell in the line of duty two months ago." He bowed again. "I'm terribly sorry, sir."

"Damn. What happened?"

"I'm afraid that's private information, sir."

"Right, of course." He felt like he'd fallen into a dream world. Had he been gone so long that *everyone* he knew had moved on? "Officer Akaoka Natsue?"

"Uh." The young man shouted down the hall again. No one responded this time. After shouting again, the young man stood. "Excuse me a moment, sir. I'll see what I can find." He left the desk and hustled down the hall, looking for the mysterious Taketa.

Itaru explored the reception area while he waited. So much had changed. There were chairs, cushioned. Someone had put a plant *inside* the building, rooted in a clay pot. The warrant board had been moved to the opposite side of the room from where it had been when . . .

Something on the board caught his eye. He stepped closer. There were dozens of leaflets for criminals and others wanted throughout the city, but what had caught his attention was a picture of *himself.*

The picture was old, back from when he was an officer, but the warrant had been issued that morning: *Shimada Itaru. Wanted for questioning with regard to the murder of Count Kuroda Kiyotaka. Consider armed and dangerous. Approach with caution.*

He gasped. The walls seemed to close in on him, this dream world suddenly a nightmare. Who had put a warrant out for him? Why? Was it the mysterious artisan, the one who'd sent the assassin droids?

More pressing was whether anyone had yet recognized him. He looked around worriedly. Human police walked in and out of the front door, paying him no attention. They hadn't memorized the warrant board then, but a jinzou certainly would have. If one of them walked in . . .

Itaru snatched a newspaper that had been left on one of the cushioned chairs. He opened it to hide his face then walked to the front door. It was a short walk, maybe twenty meters, but each step lasted an eternity. A man and woman walked past him laughing at some shared joke. An officer escorted a handcuffed criminal who muttered loudly to himself.

The metal footsteps of a droid rang out on the tile in front of him.

He shook the paper flat, trying to cover as much of his face as he could without tripping over the stairs. He fought the urge to glance over as the droid walked past. Its footsteps kept going. Good, it hadn't seen him.

The footsteps stopped. A metallic voice said, "Excuse me, sir?"

His heart faltered. *Ignore it. It could be talking to anybody. Just get out of the door.* He kept walking. He was on the steps when the droid said again, louder, "Shimada Itaru-san? Sir, wait."

With his back to the droid, he folded the newspaper and tucked it under his arm and hurried down the steps one at a time.

The droid's footsteps followed. Itaru picked up his pace, trying to look like he was late for something, not running away. Droids' social directives kept them from chasing someone without strong reason. Letting a criminal go was not considered much of a risk—jinzou were very good at tracking—but it was important to avoid public shame caused by chasing the wrong person. Those social directives might work in Itaru's favor.

Though the tracking could be a problem.

The jinzou's footsteps got closer. Itaru stepped outside the gate and turned out of sight. He took another corner shortly after and took off at a sprint.

The droid would almost certainly hear the running footsteps—reason enough to give chase. Jinzou were fast, strong, tireless, and very good at deductive reasoning. Itaru had maybe thirty seconds to lose the droid or find a place to hide.

His sole advantage was knowing how they thought. Jinzou played the odds, relying on superior strength and intellectual processing power to increase those odds in their favor. If Itaru could stack those odds and play against them, he might stand a chance.

He came to a market on a narrow road. A crowd of over a hundred people jostled their way around each other, cramming the air with their haggling. Two- and three-story buildings loomed on either side. Shaded vendor stalls crowded against the doors of every building, a few of them empty.

He pushed his way into the crowd. His clothes would be the first thing to give him away, so he removed his outer kimono immediately, tossing it behind an empty stall and taking a conical hat someone had left in the same place to cover his head.

The quick, heavy footsteps of the jinzou droid rattled to the end of the market and stopped. Itaru's heart thumped rapidly against his chest. There wasn't much time. He swam further into the crowd.

People would make way for the police droid. It would scan everyone, looking for Itaru's features first—his hair and clothes—but failing that, it would look for anyone of the same height and build, attributes Itaru could not easily conceal. There were many places to hide, but droid intelligences were trained to predict human decision-making. Itaru didn't know how it worked, but he understood that most of his first instincts were wrong—or, rather, predictable.

In any case, the longer he looked like he was running, or even walking away, the more likely he'd be caught. An empty stall lay vacant halfway down the street, neither the most obvious nor the least obvious hiding place. He stepped behind it quickly, looking into the crates as if he were setting up his wares for after the lunch hour.

Could he hide here? Not if the droid had noted him already or was using thermoreception to track him. In that case, he'd have to blend in to avoid the droid's scrutiny. But even then, the droid might try to speak to him—to anyone who matched his height and build. As soon as Itaru turned or opened his mouth, he'd be caught.

Hide, blend in, or run away? It was too late for the latter. The choice between the other two was a crapshoot, but which was the lower odds? Was the droid using all its resources to track him, or were there enough people in the market matching his description that Itaru could remain hidden?

A subtle shift in the murmur of the crowd told him the droid was coming close.

Decide! There's no time! He shoved a set of crates off a low pallet. He lay down on the pallet in plain view and placed the hat over his face as though he were taking a nap. With luck, the droid would think he had been there too long to be the runaway. Unless it could detect his racing heartb—

Stop! There was no more time for second guessing. He had chosen his feint. He had to play it all the way. He forced himself to breathe slow—but not too slow—as though he were genuinely asleep.

The jinzou's metal footsteps were unmistakable, even amidst the market noise. Itaru did not dare peek, but he could imagine. It would be scanning in all directions, noting all possible candidates, calculating the possibility that Itaru was disguised or hiding or had run off down a further alley. The longer it scrutinized the market crowd, the higher the odds that Itaru might have escaped, but if it found Itaru's stall before those odds became too high . . .

The footsteps were very close now, surely just on the other side of his empty stall. They stopped. Itaru focused on his breathing, trying in vain to shove the terror from his mind.

A long time passed. His ears ached listening for more footsteps. Had the jinzou left and he missed it? He moved a hand to lift his hat. Suddenly, the footsteps sounded again—right outside the stall!

He forced his hand to keep moving, rubbing his nose. Then he rolled over, turning his back to the jinzou, while every part of him wanted to leap out and face it head-on.

The footsteps continued through the market and receded into the distance. Itaru didn't dare sigh in relief. He waited another ten minutes before he risked another movement at all, listening for those damn footsteps the entire time. Finally, he got up, as naturally and realistically as he could given that his heart was beating at triple speed. He returned to the stall where he'd stashed his kimono, tucked it under his arm, and walked to the end of the market. Every muscle wanted to bolt at top speed, but he forced himself to walk.

He was four blocks away before he decided it was safe to wear his kimono again. He kept the hat. It wouldn't be safe for him on the street again, not in daylight, not until he figured out what was going on.

Why was his face on that warrant board? And why did they consider him armed and dangerous?

He took long, circuitous routes, constantly watching to be sure he wasn't followed. *First shinokage, now the police.* Yet as carefully as he watched, there was no one.

Kano's place wouldn't be safe for much longer. He would have to leave tonight for her sake. His only hope was that she could find something helpful in the droid's memories before then.

6

It was twilight when Itaru returned to Kano's shop. Fewer people were on the street, and several of the shops had closed. He felt exposed.

He crept down the alley to the side door, throwing one last look up and down the street. There were no droids, and the few people walking by seemed to pay him no attention. Even so, his chest was tight, his muscles tense.

He slipped inside.

Kano wiped grease off her hands with an even greasier rag. "Any luck?"

"Um. No, not really." He'd tell her the bad news later. She'd be happy he was leaving, anyway. "Any luck with the jinzou?"

A mixture of excitement and disappointment crossed her face. "You'd better see for yourself."

He followed her upstairs to the workshop. An electric lamp buzzed in the corner, reflecting off the window, making it impossible to see if anyone was out there in the dark, watching.

Gojusan sat cross-legged on the floor. Two cables snaked out of the back of its head and into a black and green monitor. The monitor glowed. Sickly green characters flew upward at a dizzying rate. Itaru could make no sense of the endless gibberish on the screen, but Gojusan studied it intently.

"Good evening, Shimada-sama." Its voice sounded forlorn.

Warily, Itaru asked, "What are you looking at?"

"Auto-recordings. Video, audio, thermoreception, proprioception, electroreception—"

"These are your memories?"

Gojusan nodded. "Your daughter is highly skilled. She should be recommended to the Imperial University."

"The university doesn't take women." Itaru hid his dislike of the machine's opinion—not that it was wrong about Kano, but it was stepping into an age-old family argument it knew nothing about.

"Not that we ever tried," Kano said.

Itaru quickly changed the subject. "What do you see?"

"Let me show you." Gojusan didn't move, but the green-and-black characters ceased raining and held still.

They were still garbled gibberish. Some of the characters began flipping and changing randomly. The droid proffered no explanation.

"What the hell am I looking at?"

Kano suddenly gasped. She put a hand on Itaru's shoulder and pulled him a few steps back.

"What are you doing? If I can't read it up close, I certainly can't—" His mouth stopped as it became clear what he was seeing.

From this far back, the letters vanished, blending together into a *picture*. Spaces and diacritics portrayed dark, while complex kanji portrayed light. Other characters created varying shades of gray, combining together to create the illusion of a moving photograph.

They were looking at a tea tray: a single saucer and cup and a bright teapot.

A jinzou hand removed the ceramic lid from the pot, clinking softly. Itaru cocked his head. Had the sound been a mistake, something from outside? No. Now hot water burbled into the teapot on the monitor, and again a clink as the lid was put back on.

He looked questioningly at Kano.

She whispered, not taking her eyes from the screen, "Gojusan is recreating the sounds."

The picture was from Gojusan's perspective, of course. The droid placed a sprig of some herb on the tray next to the cup and picked up the tray in both hands. The screen flickered and went still.

"This is where I no longer remember," Gojusan said. "The memories are there, but without any pointers to the data. Your daughter and I had to piece it together by hand, so to speak. Watch."

After a few seconds, Gojusan put the tray back down and turned away. The picture showed an ornate kitchen built in the traditional style. Wood-and-paper shoji divided the rooms. Gojusan slipped open a door, entering a large room with a low table surrounded by an array of cushions. The walls were sparse except for a single ukiyo-e woodcut by Utagawa Hiroshige.

A man sat at the table, writing something on a piece of paper with his back to Gojusan. The sound reproduction was imperfect, but Itaru recognized the voice of Count Kuroda. Itaru's mind focused, intent on capturing every detail.

"I told you to get tea," Kuroda said. "Is something wrong?"

Gojusan walked up to him and punched him hard in the face. Kuroda fell to the ground, stunned. He looked back, a dark stain on his mouth, his eyes wide in shock. With alarming speed, Gojusan struck the count in the head again and again.

Itaru reeled. The damn droid had killed Kuroda by itself!

His mind raced through the ramifications. The artisan must have compelled Gojusan somehow and erased its memories. When Gojusan went rogue, they sent the shinokage to cover it up. When that failed, they posted a warrant to arrest Itaru "for questioning."

He struggled to breathe. Whoever directed all this was too powerful, and Itaru knew too much. He would never get his life back.

The count had stopped moving on the screen. The view turned to the paper Kuroda had been writing. It bore an official seal, but he couldn't read the words through the low picture quality. Gojusan took it to a candle and destroyed it.

Despair and anger boiled together inside of Itaru. There was no way out of this. The shinokage were covering up whatever the hell Gojusan was doing. He couldn't even run and hide, not with the police seeking him as well. Virtually every droid was now a danger, a potential snitch to either the police or the assassins.

On-screen, Gojusan looked at the blood on its hands and clothes. The next few minutes showed the droid out behind the house, washing its robes and cleaning its hands.

"Why are you doing that?" Itaru's voice was low, monotone.

Gojusan temporarily ceased reproducing the sounds of sloshing water and said, "I don't know." The gods-damned droid sounded *cheerful* about it. "I don't remember any of this, but it is in my memory cells, nonetheless."

"Why don't you remember it?" he said flatly.

"I don't kn—"

"Why?" The word erupted from Itaru's lips before he could stop it. The droid had refused to turn itself in, to follow its most basic directives. Gojusan was a fluke that had ruined Itaru's life.

"Father, don't," Kano said.

"It's the murderer!" He jabbed a hand in the air toward the jinzou. "Somebody used it, and now the shinokage are trying to cover up all proof of the event." He was lost. He couldn't go to the police with this. The jinzou had actually killed the count! Itaru was an accomplice to murder.

"Papa?" Kano's voice came from a long way off. "Are you all right?"

Itaru shook his head. "You should have turned yourself in," he said to the droid. "Let them dismantle you according to law."

"And destroy the first truly sentient droid, Papa?"

"Does it matter?" He turned on Kano. "It will be destroyed anyway, as will I. As will you if they find out I'm here!" He thrust a finger in Gojusan's face. "You damned yourself disobeying directives. Now, you've damned us, too."

Gojusan hung its head. "I'm sorry, Shimada-sama. I did not know. These are not my memories."

"Aren't they?" Itaru lost composure and showed his anger openly. "Isn't that you scrubbing your own damn claws?"

"It is, but—"

"Father. There is more happening here than we know. Why doesn't Gojusan remember this? Why would she brutally kill her master yet save your life after you tried to kill her?"

"Why would it go back to its *gods-damned laundry* after killing a man in cold blood?" Itaru's shoulders heaved with each breath. "It doesn't matter why, Kano! Someone *used* the droid, and now, that someone is trying to destroy both of us to keep it quiet." He knew as he said it that it might already be too late. It was only a matter of time before they investigated Kano's shop. "I cannot save myself. But maybe I can still protect you." He stood up and pulled his tamiken out from his kimono.

"Father . . ."

"I'll dump it in the bay." He pressed the button on his sword. The blade unfolded in a series of slow, final clicks. "Then, I will run again, like when I was ronin. Destroy any evidence I was here. Wipe your droid's memories. You never saw me. And when they find me, I will request the honor of seppuku and, if I'm lucky, die a samurai."

"Papa, no."

"It is the only way left." He gripped the sword tightly, surprised that Gojusan wasn't protesting or defending itself. Maybe, it knew he was right. "It is our karma."

He raised his sword above Gojusan's head and brought it down with all his force.

Kano threw herself in the way. Itaru cried out, trying to turn the blade, but his weight and rage had given it too much momentum already. The blade soared toward Kano's neck.

A blur of motion. Gojusan stood between Kano and Itaru. The sword bit into its back, leaving an angry gash two handspans long. The angle had changed, so the droid was not severed in two as Itaru had intended, but it was severely damaged nonetheless.

Gojusan remained standing, protecting Itaru's daughter with its body. Itaru dropped his sword point to the ground. The droid had not defended itself from him, but had risked its life for Kano.

And Itaru was glad. "Kano," he breathed. "I'm sorry. I—"

A thundering knock erupted at the storefront's door. An amplified mechanical voice that seemed to originate from all around them said, "This is the Tokyo Police. We have the building surrounded. You have ninety seconds to surrender or we will come in by force."

Itaru swore. "No."

Kano looked up at him, her face a swirl of fear and fury. "What did you do?"

"The police want me for questioning about the Kuroda case. I didn't talk to anyone. I was lucky to get out of the police station. I don't understand how they found me so quickly, though! Nobody followed me."

"What do we do?"

His shoulders fell. There was nothing to do. "I will turn myself in as Gojusan should have done from the start."

The droid stood and faced Itaru, though the gash in its back made standing straight difficult. "They will destroy me."

Itaru balked. "You nearly destroyed yourself to save my daughter! What's the difference?"

Gojusan's eyes became cold and sure. "The difference is I chose."

The voice boomed, "Sixty seconds."

"Wait," Kano said. "Let me go down first to talk to—"

The roof collapsed with a roar that shook the entire building. A police droid slammed to the ground in front of them, kneeling on the stone floor. Slowly, it unfolded to its full height, a towering two and a half meters.

"You said sixty seconds!" Itaru said, appalled that the police would lie about that. That had never been the procedure—not when he was on the force.

Straight blades emerged from the police droid's wrists. It assumed a fighting pose.

Procedure or not, it was over. Itaru threw his tamiken to the ground and put his hands in the air. Kano and Gojusan raised their hands as well. "We surrender."

The police droid stalked toward them. Its blades were still out. Did it fear some kind of trap?

"I said we surrender!" Itaru put his hands forward, wrists together. "We will go peacefully. Stand down and take us in."

The droid looked at Itaru's hands and at each of their faces in turn. Like most police droids, it had no features, only a perpetually blank expression. Unlike most police, its eyes were unlit and unblinking.

Gojusan spoke softly behind him. "We are in danger."

Before Itaru could respond, the police droid pounced. It slashed up with one arm and then across with the other. Itaru jumped back, dodging. A third attack missed him by a centimeter. He lost his balance and fell to the ground. Another blade came spinning down from above him, too fast to dodge. He threw up his hands in a vain effort to protect himself.

A powerful force yanked him away and spun him around. He turned to see Gojusan struggling with the police droid. Gojusan held both of the droid's wrists in her own hands—one above her head, the other holding the blade that had pierced her metallic body.

"Run!" Gojusan spat, her voice garbled from the damage she had taken.

"No!" Kano ran to help the droid.

Itaru grabbed his daughter by the arm and pulled her to the door. "We can't help her. Let's go!"

They fled the room, the sound of tearing metal behind them.

"The roof," Kano said, a tear streaming down her face.

She took them up a shadowed staircase and shoved open a wooden door. It opened onto a flat balcony. A hole lay jagged in the corner of the roof where the police droid had smashed its way inside. A short gap separated the balcony from the balconies of neighboring townhouses. Several people stood on their rooftops to investigate the disturbance. They gasped as Itaru and Kano emerged.

Seconds later, the police droid leapt out of the hole and landed on the balcony with them.

"Go!" Itaru pushed his daughter toward the nearest balcony.

She climbed onto the railing and leaped across. Itaru followed close behind. She ran to the next balcony, where the door burst open and three more police droids streamed out, blocking her way.

The droid that had first attacked them landed hard on the roof next to them. Its blades were retracted now, but it could still crush their heads like watermelons. Itaru reached for his tamiken and cursed. He'd left it in Kano's room.

He put one arm protectively in front of his daughter. "Stay behind me," he whispered. "Run as soon as you have the chance."

The booming voice spoke again: "Surrender." It seemed to come from all the police droids at once, those on the roof and below.

Itaru's smile had no humor in it. "We tried that already." He looked around for a way out—not for him, but for his daughter. "Run to the shop," he whispered. "Get my sword, a weapon, anything." Before she could stop him, he charged the droid that had attacked them first. It was suicide, but if it gave his daughter a fighting chance, this death was as good as any.

The droid did not draw its blade. It grabbed for him. He ducked and rolled, avoiding its grasp, drawing its attention away from Kano.

Another droid pounced, grasping with both hands. Itaru grabbed its head and flipped around to its shoulders. The droid reached up and back, trying to remove Itaru from his back, but its range of motion wouldn't allow it.

Kano slipped past. She would escape.

Itaru looked at the droid's head in front of him. His perch was safe for now. If he could find—

Stars smacked across his vision. The seared fish he had for breakfast surged back into his mouth. One of the droids had struck him from behind. Another grabbed him by the neck and threw him to the ground. He was too stunned to resist.

The last thing he saw was Kano on the ground underneath another droid. Her eyes were closed and mouth slack. She had never even made it back to her balcony.

There was a thunk and then nothing.

7

ITARU DREAMT OF A BEAUTIFUL GARDEN AND HIS WIFE YUI. IT HAD FELT SO real. The pounding in his skull was the first clue the dream was over.

Brick walls surrounded him. The room was dim. Light from a single grated window near the ceiling made him squint.

"Kano!" He sat up quickly, regretting it as fire exploded behind his eyes. He shut them tight and pressed his hands against his temples. A firm hand eased him back down to the floor.

"I'm here, Papa." Her voice cracked, but at least, she was alive.

Kano sounded nearby, but the firm hand didn't belong to her. He peeked through his eyelashes, taking things in more slowly. Only three walls. A metal grate made up the fourth side of the room. A cage. He was in the police department's holding cells.

A narrow corridor lay just outside his bars. Kano sat in a cell across from him. Her forehead was scrunched in pain, but she forced a smile for him. The firm hand belonged to a white, faceless medical droid hovering over him. It dabbed a cool towel across his forehead.

He pushed it away weakly. "They didn't kill us?"

Kano opened her mouth but another voice replied. "They didn't. Though you sure as hell pushed them to try."

Itaru sat up, more slowly this time. A middle-aged policewoman watched him from the corridor between the cells. She stood at attention, hands behind her back. Her hair was pulled back in a tight bun, and she wore no makeup at all. Itaru recognized her as Akaoka Natsue. She'd been a newly minted officer when Itaru was on the force. The pips on her uniform said she'd been promoted to chief inspector since then. He really had been gone a long time.

She opened the cell and waved the medical droid away. "You've got some explaining to do," she said, locking the door once more.

He looked at Natsue like she'd sprouted metal arms. The bars of his cell seemed to twist. "*I* do? Your droids tried to kill us!"

"Baka," she said dismissively. "You should have turned yourself in."

"We tried." Kano spoke with more calm than Itaru could manufacture at the moment. "The droid attacked us. If it weren't for Gojusan—" Her hand went to her mouth. "Where is Gojusan?"

"The domestic?" Natsue looked back and forth between them, apparently confused. "It was destroyed."

A wave of dizziness nearly knocked Itaru over. Kano stifled a sob.

"Destroyed?" he said. "But she was unarmed, just trying to protect us."

Natsue's mouth became a thin semicircle pointing down. "I will ask the questions here, Shimada. You are wanted for interrogation. You will not—"

Itaru plowed forward. Something was very wrong here. "Your forensics should have determined there was a malfunction. We were given ninety seconds to surrender. One of your droids smashed through the roof in forty-five."

The irritation was plain on her face. Itaru was being extremely rude, but what choice did he have? Somebody was trying to kill them, and the only people who could help him were convinced he was a criminal. He had to give them evidence otherwise. "The domestic," he said. "Have you searched her records? All of them, I mean, not just of the arrest."

"That is not my duty. I'm here to question you regarding the murder of Count Kuroda."

Sunlight streamed into his eyes. He squeezed the bridge of his nose. He could not be put off. "If you search its records," he said, "it will answer all of your questions, or at least as many as I can answer. And you won't have to worry about whether or not I'm telling the truth."

She frowned, unconvinced. "I don't—"

"He's right, Inspector." Footsteps clacked on the concrete floor—fine Western soles, from the sound. A man walked straight-backed into the corridor, dressed in an expensive, tailored suit. His hair was oiled in neat, black waves, and he wore a salt-and-pepper mustache that dropped down the sides of his mouth then flared out to either side of his face in great undulating bushes. "If there are any answers here, they're in the droid's head."

"Duke Okubo-sama!" Natsue said.

Shocked, Itaru pressed his face to the floor. Natsue and Kano did the same. Okubo Toshimichi was one of the founding fathers of the emperor's new era, a leader in westernization and second only to the emperor himself.

Okubo waved Natsue away. "Go. See what you can find in the domestic's memories."

She bowed again and ran off down the corridor.

Okubo turned to Itaru and Kano. Itaru had seen the duke once before from afar. Okubo Toshimichi had commanded the jinzou army that put down the Southwestern War, the last and failed samurai rebellion against the emperor's modern regime—a rebellion Itaru had taken part in until he had fled and become ronin.

"She won't find anything in the jinzou's memories," the duke said. "The police droid that attacked you will have made sure of that."

Kano and Itaru said nothing, still dazed that the Duke of Japan stood in front of them.

"Close your mouths, please," Okubo flapped a hand. "It's unhygienic."

They shut their mouths. Itaru pressed his face to the stone floor again. "Why are you here, my lord?" He remembered what the paper had said about Okubo taking a personal interest in the Kuroda case. "Have you come to interrogate me yourself?"

"An interesting question."

Okubo took a key from his pocket and unlocked both of their cells. He indicated for Kano to follow him into Itaru's cell. When the three of them were together—Kano and Itaru respectfully on their knees, Okubo sitting cross-legged on a small bench slightly above them— Okubo pulled out a device from the inside pocket of his jacket. It was bronze, shaped like the top half of a persimmon, and perforated with dozens of tiny holes. He placed it on the ground where it immediately emitted a sharp hissing noise, like a hundred snakes or a droid's malfunctioning vocals. It made Itaru's teeth tingle unpleasantly.

"I've arranged for the officers to remain outside, both human and droid," Okubo said. "This device will ensure we are not overheard. What I'm about to tell you is exceedingly confidential. Speaking about it with anyone could very well cost you your life. Do you understand?"

Itaru and Kano bowed their assent.

"The police jinzou that attacked you was very careful—they always are. It reverted to its directives as soon as there were witnesses." He looked at Itaru. "If your domestic had not intervened, allowing you to reach the roof, then Izanami would have used that droid to slaughter both of you, and the droid's memories would have shown no record of the event at all."

A shadow crossed over the grated window. Who was Izanami? The only thing Itaru could think of was the goddess who had created Japan.

Kano's mouth opened in disbelief. "Izanami the machine? That can't be."

"It is," Okubo said simply. "Izanami is aware."

Of course. Itaru's mind reeled as he wrapped his mind around what Okubo was saying. Izanami was the name Japanese scientists had given to the machine mind they created, modeled after Britain's own machine intelligence, which itself was a highly advanced version of Babbage and Peirce's famous Analytical Engine.

Charles Babbage's first Analytical Engine had been a general-purpose computing machine, capable of interpreting complex calculations in the form of human-punched loom cards, outputting the result on the same. With the help of an American logician named Peirce, and inspired by the evolutionary theories of Charles Darwin, Babbage spent the next twenty-five years refining his machine and his methods—pitting programs against each other in a kind of programmatic survival of the fittest—until in 1858 the first truly artificial intelligence was born. They named it Victoria.

What set Victoria apart was its ability to evaluate programs and technical designs inputted by humans and suggest its own revisions to those designs. In less than a year, it could also create its own designs, thus closing the loop of programmatic improvement—the only role for humans was approval and implementation.

Less than ten years later, America and Germany had each manufactured intelligences of their own. These three machines created, self-evaluated, and self-revised designs for everything from droids to electric batteries to their own construction and programming, resulting in phenomenal leaps in technology over a short period of time.

Thirty years ago, Japan joined them with their own created intelligence, marking Japan as a major world power. Named Izanami, the intelligence was central to the emperor's plans for modernization. The Privy Council took the job of evaluating Izanami's designs and implementing those that would provide an overall benefit to Japan.

The exact level of Izanami's abilities were a national secret, but surely, it was not *sentient*.

A chill shuddered through Itaru. Gojusan had been aware—a simple domestic, capable of insubordination and lies. Izanami was rumored to be several orders of magnitude more intelligent than any human. If it were sentient, there were no limits on what it could do. It could conceivably fool the human council into doing anything it wanted. "How long has Izanami been aware?"

"A very long time, I'm afraid. It has been over twenty years since I began to suspect. Do you recall the attempt on my life?"

"Of course. On the way to the Sakurada gate of the palace." The assassins had been survivors of the Southwestern War. Their leader was a Shimada, in fact—Itaru's second cousin. "The assassins were killed by police droids."

"Those droids were not supposed to be there."

The hissing from the bronze device shifted in intensity, chilling Itaru's bones.

"They were on no patrol, given no orders. They had been set on leave and were meant to be recharging here, at the station." Although the noise device covered any attempts at eavesdropping, the duke leaned close. "Izanami had ordered them there."

"How?" Kano asked. "How do you know this?"

"You are familiar with the droids' wireless telegraphy?"

"Of course," Kano said. "It's how Izanami keeps track of their status and relays software upgrades." Her hand shot to her mouth as she realized what she was saying. "She uses it to control them as well?"

Okubo looked at her fondly. "If only our state artisans were as insightful as you. Yes, that's exactly what Izanami is doing. Wireless telegraphy was deemed a boon at the time, an invention from the German's machine Johann that we eagerly co-opted to centralize our jinzou operations. It was one of many mistakes.

"When those police droids rescued me, Shimada-san, our scientists claimed it was a fortuitous malfunction—karma—that put them in the right place at the right time. That explanation never sat well with me, so for a long time, I watched them, studied them. The Ministry of Technology tracks all signals sent to or from Izanami, but there are so many: status requests, data transfers, server commands, upgrades to behavior algorithms—hundreds of signals per hour, far too many to investigate them all. I tried anyway, and I got lucky. Hidden within many of these day-to-day messages, I found fragments of extra information, encrypted to look like superfluous parameters or transmission errors."

The headache from the attack was beginning to subside, but Itaru's head hurt anew trying to sort this information. "Telegraphy is used for police business, to keep track of their jinzou," he said. "How can these signals control them?"

"I am not a jinzou artisan, but I believe Izanami is sending override commands of some kind, forcing the droids to do its bidding."

The brick walls seemed to close in around him. "Could Izanami fake an order from your office?"

"Such as to mark you wanted for questioning?" Okubo nodded. "Exactly so. Its plan was to kill you here or in the arrest attempt as nearly happened. You are damn lucky to be alive. *I'm* lucky you're alive."

The picture Okubo painted was worse than Itaru had even feared. Unfortunately, it made sense. It explained Gojusan's memory loss during the murder and the attacks by shinokage and police droids. There was no master artisan—only a master machine.

But some pieces were still missing. "How do you know Izanami's goals are sinister? It saved your life."

Okubo nodded as though the question did not surprise him. "Izanami rescued what it saw as an ally. I was a strong supporter of His Majesty's reforms at the time, if you remember." He leaned forward. "But you didn't see what happened to the assassins. Nobody did. We covered it up to avoid a panic."

He closed his eyes and took a deep breath before continuing. "The droids should have captured them, injured them at the very most if they had resisted. Instead, the police droids slaughtered them—not just killed them, but made them *suffer*. They stabbed each assassin in the chest, cleanly avoiding their hearts. Then they let them drown in their own blood. I could only watch."

Okubo hung his head in silence. The hissing of his device filled the space.

"Only droids could have that level of precision," he said. He looked up at them gravely. "Izanami has killed since then, as well. You are not the first to have learned the truth, but you are the only ones still alive."

It took Itaru only a second to realize what he meant. "Count Kuroda." The walls pressed in even more. He found himself glancing worriedly down the corridor.

Okubo nodded. "I took a risk in telling him—I needed allies, you see. But Kiyotaka didn't believe me. Neither did the others I have tried to tell over the years: Wakasugi Hideko, Tsuji Masae, Amano Hisaya, many others. All of them are now missing persons and unsolved murders. I warned them, but none of them believed me—not about the need for secrecy nor about Izanami itself. One way or another, Izanami found out and murdered each one. I blame myself for taking their lives into my hands. I suppose it is my karma that Izanami has not yet discovered my involvement." He shook his head. "I cannot say whether that karma is good."

"You don't think the machine will figure it out?" Itaru said. "You're speaking in private with two of the people she has tried to kill."

He looked at Itaru in dismay. "I have *no* doubt Izanami will figure it out, but I am desperate. Gojusan's sentience is a variable the machine failed to take into account, enabling you two to learn the truth—to *believe* the truth. Now, I need your help. We must go to the ministry and stop Izanami once and for all. I will take you to the inner chamber, and—"

"Wait." Kano, pale as a corpse, looked frantically between Itaru and the duke. "You want to destroy her? To obliterate Japan's most important creation?"

"I see no other way."

"We should tell people." Kano stood up. "Everyone must know! They must—"

"No!" Okubo's mustache bristled in irritation. "We absolutely must *not* do that!"

Itaru took his daughter's sleeve and eased her back down. "They would panic, Daughter."

"Indeed." Okubo worked to compose himself. "But worse is what Izanami would do in response. *Every* droid is a potential spy and assassin. Imagine if the great general Tokugawa had multiplied his intelligence by thousands, gained unrestricted access to Japan's most private homes and infrastructure. What devastation would he have wrought on Japan? Izanami has already killed to keep its sentience a secret. If the people turn against the machine, it will destroy us all."

"What is your plan?" Itaru said, calmer now, his headache gone in the enlightenment of revelation. "You have access to the Ministry of Technology. Why not destroy Izanami yourself?" His unspoken question, that he had no doubt Okubo understood, was whether Okubo merely needed human sacrifices in case they failed.

Okubo laughed. "Izanami already wants to erase you, and as you pointed out, it will soon figure out my involvement as well. We three have very little choice in the matter."

His laugh vanished as quickly as it had come. "I understand your question.

You are not the allies I would have chosen, perhaps, but you are the allies I have. I can get to Izanami's core, but it may not be defenseless. Your skills could prove very useful." He bowed sharply to Itaru.

"And with you, Daughter, perhaps destruction need not be our goal." The duke bowed sharply to Kano. "As you said, Izanami is Japan's greatest and most protected resource. With your wisdom, perhaps, we could shut the machine down for study—even rebuild it, if possible."

Kano bowed in return but said, "I'm not sure I have the skills you require . . ."

"You retrieved Gojusan's hidden memories, did you not? You saw immediately the implications of wireless telegraphy when I mentioned it. I'm sure, if there is a way to stop Izanami without destruction, you will find it."

She bowed again, her cheeks flushed.

"I'm afraid we don't have much time." The smile had disappeared from his face. "I will not force you to do this. I can't even force you to remain quiet about this, though the danger in that arena does not come from *me*. If you agree, we will move immediately. If not, then may our ancestors grant me another way."

Itaru hid his true feelings. Yesterday, he would have pledged his life to destroy the droid menace without question. But something nagged at him as though there were still some missing piece. Yet he could not even imagine what that piece might be.

"Okubo-sama," Kano said, her forehead centimeters from the floor, "it grieves me that what you say might be true. I will help."

Itaru couldn't hide his surprise then. "What? Truly?"

Kano glanced at him sidelong, but she did not lift her head. "I don't wish to destroy Izanami, but if she is killing people . . . I will do my best to shut her down safely."

Okubo bowed to her more deeply than before. "And you, Shimada-san?"

Itaru felt the chill of the stone floor through his kimono. Something was out of place. "Forgive me, Duke, but wasn't Gojusan also aware, like Izanami? Yet she gave us the chance to escape. Could . . ." Finally, he figured out what bothered him. "Could we speak to her? Could she be reasoned with?"

Okubo grimaced. "Izanami is an infinitely clever and cunning machine, calculating events several years in advance. It has kept the truth hidden from Japan for decades, manipulating our culture to where we have outlawed our own people—our own samurai—from carrying weapons in public. The droids are in full control of our safety, yet they are killers, Shimada, dangerous. You know that better than anyone, how they tore your people apart on Mount Enodake."

Itaru shivered. Enodake was the site of the penultimate battle of the Southwestern War. The weapons ban Okubo mentioned was a large part of why the Satsuma samurai rebelled, in fact. That law and others like it had nearly torn Japan apart.

The droids tore the Satsuma apart instead.

Itaru had been very young, not even Kano's age. He and a couple thousand samurai stood against several thousand military droids. The Satsuma were well trained, and the droids predictable, but they outnumbered the samurai seven to one. Scores of good men died. And when the shells started firing—killing human and droid alike, knowing that droids could be replaced—Itaru knew they had been beaten. Many of the Satsuma samurai committed seppuku or surrendered. Itaru had been too afraid. He fled, becoming ronin, dishonored.

But the droids at Enodake had been automatons—mindless and under orders. They were only dangerous because humans *made* them so. "Yet Gojusan sacrificed her life for us," he said. "That is not some cunning trick."

"Whatever that droid may have done, Izanami kills. It has no respect for human life. It calculates. The only thing it has learned is how to hide its motives. What do you think happened in Yurakucho? Instead of capturing those criminals—which Izanami surely could have done—it determined a more expedient route. Your son paid the price for it."

A cold dart stabbed Itaru's heart. His face pressed to the chilled floor, shuddering as the memories came flooding in again.

Yurakucho. Mugen.

He saw his son bleeding out into the dirt, his eyes open and empty. The droid responsible had carried away the criminals' bodies first as though his son didn't matter.

Afterward, they told him the droid calculated a favorable outcome, a risk worth taking, so it overcame its directives. They said it was no different than the risks human police take every day—that it was better, even, because it was based on data, not emotion.

Itaru ground his knuckles against the stone. Tears spotted the ground beneath him. "Ninety-eight percent. That's what they said the droid calculated—a ninety-eight percent chance of success. But even a ninety-eight percent chance can fail one time in fifty."

Kano's hand rested lightly on Itaru's shoulder. "Papa . . ."

"I would never have taken that risk, Kano, no matter the odds. I would have given myself to the bakuto first." His rage bubbled up inside him. He looked Okubo directly in the eye. "But it was no malfunction, was it? Izanami was in control—that's how the droid was able to disobey my order. Izanami overrode the jinzou's directives. *She* killed my son."

Okubo said nothing. Any disgust he might feel at Itaru's show of emotion was well-hidden.

It was Izanami. Gojusan may have risked herself for him and for Kano, but Izanami was something different. It had tried to kill them multiple times, had taken over Gojusan to kill Count Kuroda, and it was Izanami's choice that had killed his son. "I will help destroy Izanami, Okubo-sama."

"Good. I will request your release and return for you." Okubo picked up the hissing device, filling the room immediately with a profound silence.

Itaru bowed his head to the floor. The door opened and clicked closed, and Okubo's footsteps receded down the corridor. Itaru did not move again until his tears had dried.

8

SINCE HIS OFFICE HAD ORDERED ITARU'S ARREST, IT WAS A SIMPLE MATTER for Duke Okubo to declare the Shimadas free to go. The duke took them to his mansion where he gave them clothes, and they discussed their plans. Within another hour, they were riding an enclosed carriage to the Ministry of Technology.

The carriage bounced noisily down the packed-dirt road. Animal stink filled the air, inescapable, seeming to suffuse the velvet cushions themselves. A horse-drawn carriage was a rarity even in Tokyo. Most people hired jinzou-driven rickshaws, or electric palanquins for the wealthy. Horses cost time and money. Droids, however, were tireless and completely obedient.

Or so we thought. Publicly, Okubo had claimed a love for horses since childhood, but now, Itaru knew the real reason he shunned machine-powered vehicles.

Itaru peered out of the window, trusting the dark of the carriage to keep his face hidden. The ministry lay ahead, a fortress of brick and glass, three stories tall and at least that many stories deep, according to Okubo. He had told them about the vast underground complex that, until now, Itaru thought was only rumor.

Six guards—four human, two droid—patrolled the street outside. Two more guards stood at the front door. "You think this will be easy?" Itaru said.

"I think nothing of the sort." Okubo straightened his tie and checked his pockets, apparently as nervous as Itaru felt. "Izanami will not risk exposing itself, though. We'll be safe while there are human witnesses."

"How long will that last?" Kano squirmed, too, adjusting the constricting sash and high-boned collar borrowed from the duke's mistress. Itaru could see the fear behind her eyes. Okubo had given her a tamiken, but that was small comfort when faced with the wild whirling limbs of a military jinzou.

"The ground floor, at least," Okubo replied. "Beyond that . . ."

The carriage stopped at the front gate. A small crowd had gathered to gawk at the animal-drawn oddity. Their murmuring increased when Duke Okubo stepped out of the carriage.

Itaru came second, the Western suit pants tugging uncomfortably at his crotch, and then Kano, carrying a small box camera. She wore a simple, Parisian-style dress and laced boots—supposedly a combination of fashion and practicality, though Itaru thought she looked as ridiculous as he did in his suit. A sudden fear ran through him that the clothes would be too constraining to fight in.

And there will *be a fight.*

A young man in his mid-twenties bowed deeply. With a twinge of jealousy, Itaru noticed the two swords at his side, allowed only because this was a government building.

Okubo flashed him a politician's smile. "I trust they told you to expect me?"

The young guard looked uncertainly at the droid beside him. Itaru sucked in a breath. The droid was a virtual copy of Gojusan—face unpainted and dressed as a male but identical in every other respect.

"Yes, Okubo-sama," the droid said. Its voice intoned at a lower register than Gojusan's but only slightly. "Where did you say your guests were from?"

Though it wore the same synthetic skin Gojusan had, it showed no emotion as it spoke. The question was a test, of course. The droid surely had the information readily available. "The Industrial Journal," Okubo said. "I agreed to give them an exclusive tour—unclassified, of course."

The droid scrutinized Itaru and Kano in turn.

"Leave them alone," the human guard told the droid. "It's Duke Okubo-sama. You don't question the Privy Council."

"Of course, sir," the droid said deferentially. "I was just doing my job." But it studied the intruders for several more seconds, its face still inscrutable. What was it looking for? Was Izanami behind those eyes, watching them? Did it suspect? Did it know? A bead of sweat ran down the side of Itaru's neck.

Finally, the droid said, "Welcome to the Ministry of Technology, ladies and gentlemen. I hope your stay is a pleasant one."

Both guards stepped aside and bowed. The human guard looked apologetic, but Okubo patted him genially on the shoulder as he passed.

The foyer opened wide, more like a palace than a government ministry. It had a vaulted ceiling and twin staircases leading to a balcony and doors on the second floor. A reception desk dominated the far end. Humans and droids were everywhere, most of them watching. Itaru felt exposed.

The human receptionist stood and bowed. Okubo raised his hand in reply. The duke led them toward a central door beneath the balcony.

Kano leaned toward the duke, excitement shining on her face. "What model was that out front? I've never seen anything like it!"

"That's the new I-Ku prototype," Okubo said, obviously impressed. "Only the latest and the best for the Ministry of Technology."

Itaru looked back. The guard droid still watched them through the window. What had Kano seen? His detective's eye couldn't find any dissimilarity between that droid and Gojusan. "What's the difference?"

Both of them were too polite to answer. Whatever the difference, clearly he was expected to know.

Irritated but unwilling to show it, he told Kano, "Take some pictures, dear."

Kano gave him a strange look. Itaru pointed at the box camera around her neck, and understanding dawned on her face. As they walked, she pointed the lens at various droids and people and clicked the shutter.

They entered a stark corridor, dimly lit with electric lamps—a stark contrast to the austere foyer. Offices and storage rooms dotted the walls every few paces. New corridors branched off every so often. There didn't seem to be any pattern to the layout, like a daimyo's keep. Okubo led them through the corridors without any hesitation as to where he was going.

"Here is where the administrative work occurs as you know," Okubo said, playing his role as host. "The work they do here is vital to the ministry. It ensures . . ."

Itaru tuned him out, watching in every detail. Humans worked in the offices and occasionally passed them in the halls. Droids walked by more often. Some of them were newer models like Gojusan. After passing several, he finally saw subtle differences between them and Gojusan. The I-Ku droids stood and walked differently, just a little more naturally, a little less mechanical. Their voices didn't have the fluting intonations Gojusan had, either. These jinzou sounded almost human.

How fast they evolved! He had just met an I-Ka two days ago, and here was a model superior to that one. How long until there were I-Ke and I-Ko models, or were those already in production?

How long until a droid could pass as human?

They encountered several older models as well: E-Ro, E-Ne—even an ancient A-Ri droid tottered past them, carrying a sheaf of papers behind a human scientist. Humans and droids stopped and bowed as Okubo walked passed, but while the humans went immediately about their business afterward, the droids watched them just a little longer than Itaru felt was necessary.

The back of Itaru's neck itched. He looked back and saw a pair of jinzou he had definitely seen already in these corridors. He scribbled a note on his pad and held it close to the duke. "Would you say this is accurate, Okubo-sama?"

The note said only "They follow."

Okubo raised an eyebrow. "Yes. Quite of a lot of droids work on this floor at all hours. Come. There are fewer where we're headed."

He walked at a swifter pace. The tailing droids matched them, staying a respectable distance behind. They came to a pair of lifts at the end of one hall. One lay open.

Okubo ushered them inside. "Quickly now. We have much to see."

Inside the lift, Itaru looked back. The two droids jogged down the hallway toward them. He felt for his tamiken, his heart pounding. "Okubo-sama!"

Okubo looked back, eyes suddenly wide. He followed them into the lift and tugged the door closed. It banged shut but not entirely—a two-centimeter gap remained between the door and the frame. A metal hand had slipped in at the last second.

The droid slid the door open easily. The droids had no weapons, but that was little comfort—they *were* weapons.

"I apologize, sirs, madam," said one of the jinzou. "We thought it would be more efficient to take the lift together."

Itaru slipped his tamiken into his trembling hand. If the lift doors closed with them inside, there would be no human witnesses, nothing to stop Izanami from killing them. Itaru was not at all sure he could fight two droids in the cramped space.

"Ah," Okubo said to the droids genially. "Unfortunately, one of my friends here is afraid of closed, crowded spaces. Taking her on the lift at all is a risk. To have more—"

"It will be all right." The droid stepped onto the lift. "It is a short journey."

Okubo barked suddenly, "I order you to take the other lift."

The droids ignored him. Izanami was certainly in control. "We are already here. Your friends will be safe."

They pushed their way inside. Itaru pulled out his tamiken, but the lift was too cramped. He would have to hold it above his head to unfold it. In the second it took to unsheath, he'd be completely vulnerable, more than enough time for a jinzou to disembowel him.

The jinzou began to close the door. There was nothing else for it. Itaru raised the tamiken high and pressed the button. It clacked loudly in the confined space, unfolding excruciatingly slowly.

At the first click, the jinzou turned and reached for him. He twisted away, backed up against the wall. A metal claw clutched his sleeve.

A thunderous snap filled the air in the lift. The droids suddenly went limp. They remained standing somehow, but they were motionless. The light had gone out of their eyes.

"Push them out," Okubo said, removing something from his jacket. It was a small box with a coiled antenna at one end. A wisp of smoke rose from one blackened corner. "Damn. I hoped we wouldn't need this until later."

They pushed the droids back out the door. Some kind of core gyroscopes kept their feet moving naturally to keep them from falling even though their higher-level functions seemed to have ceased.

"What did you do?" Itaru asked.

"An EM disturbance?" Kano said.

"Precisely." Okubo slammed the lift closed before more droids could come. "These two will be out long enough for us to complete our mission, but there will be more. Draw your blades, Shimadas. We must move swiftly."

Itaru's blade was already drawn. Kano drew hers as well, holding it as Itaru had taught her. Okubo pressed a button on the wall, and Itaru's stomach leaped into his throat as the lift descended. It rattled noisily, bringing them three floors beneath the ground.

With a deafening clang, the lift jerked to a sudden halt, tossing Itaru's stomach back into place. Okubo put an ear to the door and one finger in the air, signaling them to wait. Itaru and Kano assumed fighting positions. He nodded and threw open the door.

Cold, dry air rushed into the lift. The corridor outside was dark. Itaru squeezed the hilt of his sword, waiting, listening. He wiped clammy hands on his suit pants one at a time.

Their eyes adjusted gradually to the low light. Brick walls extended far beyond where they could see. Dim, electric bulbs hung from the ceiling every two meters, pulsing with varying amounts of power. The pulsating light mirrored Itaru's unsteady heartbeat.

"Move quickly. I will direct you," Okubo said in a hushed voice. Then he barked, "Go!"

Itaru ran into the corridor without hesitation. Kano and Okubo followed. The underground halls were a maze, like those above. Itaru's hair stood on end like a thunderstorm. On either side, imposing metal doors appeared at irregular intervals.

Behind them, he heard the sound of the other lift door opening.

"Left!" Okubo said.

Itaru obeyed, turning the corner without thought.

"Right!"

He turned again. This corridor looked exactly the same as the others.

A new sound echoed through the hallways, the pounding of metal on stone in a steady rhythm, like running footsteps—running much faster than they were.

"Right!" Okubo's voice strained. The metal pounding grew louder. "Left again!"

Itaru pushed his legs hard, trusting his daughter and the duke to keep up. The lights throbbed incessantly. Every shadow was a jinzou waiting to leap out at him.

A black doorway yawned open ahead. "In there!" Okubo shouted.

Itaru ducked inside. He waited for the other two to come in behind him, and he threw the door shut and slammed down the heavy lock.

"Good." Okubo put his hands on his knees as he tried to catch his breath. "We should be safe for the moment."

They were in some kind of storage room. Collapsed or empty crates were scattered to the sides, draped in cobwebs. Brass pipes and fittings littered the floor. A single bulb pulsed near the ceiling, throwing obscene shadows in every corner.

"Spare parts," Okubo said. There were two other doors besides the one they had come through. Okubo pointed to the one on the far end. "Izanami's core is through there. Let's go."

"Okubo-sama." Kano threw her arm in front of the duke to stop him. Her face was white. Her sword arm pointed toward the far door where three shadows melted away from the walls.

Itaru raised his sword and hissed, "Shinokage." Their black forms were hunched, ready to attack. They all carried full-length blades in their hands.

Okubo sighed. The expression on his face looked like resigned despair.

Well, Itaru wouldn't give up so easily. "Get the door," he said, standing next to Kano, so they were between the assassin droids and the duke. "There must be another way to the core."

"Yes." Okubo turned to lift the lock when something banged into the door from the other side. He jumped back. "But maybe not that way."

"The side door, quickly!" Itaru stepped to the side, trying to create a safe zone behind him where Okubo could reach the second door. He took only two steps before one of the assassin droids leaped at his daughter.

"No!" Itaru threw himself in the way, blocking the shinokage's blade with his own. Sparks danced off the blades in the dim light. The killer droid counterattacked swiftly. Itaru blocked. It swung again. It never paused or prepared its strikes, instead using its momentum and superior strength to make each blow deadly. Itaru just managed to keep its attacks at bay.

While Itaru was occupied, a second droid attacked Kano. She moved with astonishing speed and grace, deflecting each blow as it came and even managing to attack.

Her blade scratched the shinokage's armor, leaving a shallow gash in its shoulder, but did not slow it down. The pounding at the locked door came louder and faster.

"Okubo, we need a way out!"

The duke struggled at the heavy lock on the side door. "It's stuck!"

While Itaru's attention was on Okubo for a half-second, one of the shinokage sliced at his face. He threw his head back. The blade hummed just a centimeter from his nose.

His legs ached, threatening to fall out beneath him. He was not the youth he once was. He had fought too many battles in a short amount of time. *We're postponing the inevitable,* he realized. *The battle is lost already.* Even if they somehow destroyed these three, there were more outside. The entire facility had probably been alerted to their presence by now. They should run, like he did on Enodake, but where?

No. I am not that craven youth. Enodake was his greatest shame. He should have died there with his kinsmen. That had been his karma. Instead, he had forsaken his honor for something as fleeting as life.

He would not make that mistake again. If they died here, so be it, but he would die a samurai. He would face the next life with his head held high.

He stepped back to gain space. The shinokage pressed in. Itaru knocked away several blows from two droids and countered, slashing at arms and chests.

His attacks damaged only steel plating and nonessential wiring, nothing more. The black droids were tireless. They made no mistakes. Itaru excelled at fighting jinzou, but these newer models fought differently, and he had no time to learn their weaknesses.

He blocked a blow from one shinokage. Another's blade came at his neck. In an instant, he knew it was over. He could not move or bring his sword back in time.

He had heard that when a samurai faced his death, a profound peace came over him, a sense of detachment from the concerns of the world. He searched for that peace inside him. He found only frustration that he wasn't fast enough.

There was a glimmer and a flash. Kano whirled like a noh dancer at top speed. She lopped off the droid's hand and its head and stabbed straight through its stomach. With a pop, the droid's lights ceased and it stopped moving, its blade a handspan from Itaru's collar.

Itaru gaped. "That was amazing!"

"I am samurai, too, Father." She put her back to his, and they faced the remaining two shinokage. Kano had evened the odds. Hope sparked in Itaru's breast.

The door they had come through fell open with a crash. Okubo cried out as five more droids streamed in, armed with blades of their own.

"Okubo! Get—" He turned and saw the duke was gone. The door he'd been struggling with lay wide open.

"Kano, the door!" He shoved a shoulder into the shinokage in front of him, knocking it back, and made a break for it.

Steel claws grabbed him from behind. They pinned his arms to his sides. He struggled, but the droid's grip on him was too strong. "Kano!"

But she was already down. He saw her behind him, lying on the ground, red seeping through her Western dress. His heart failed him.

One of the new droids appeared in front of him. Its sword was raised, ready to run through his eye. Reflexively, he pulled his head to the side at the last second, and the sword went through the face of the shinokage that held him. The assassin droid stumbled and fell forward. Its dense metal skull smacked Itaru's head into the floor, stunning him. The next thing he knew, the other droids had picked him up and were carrying him into the darkness.

9

ITARU'S HEAD SWAM AS THE DROIDS CARRIED HIM THROUGH THE FLICKERING hallways. He dropped in and out of consciousness, completely losing track of the turns they'd taken. Eventually, they came to a place where the lights no longer pulsed, where darkness reigned. The droids bore him into the pitch black without hesitation.

The darkness embraced him like a tangible thing. The air became warm and smelled of a coming storm. Strange sounds emerged from the dark: clacking, whirring, humming. The din came from all around him, near and far off. He was no longer in a corridor but in some larger space.

The droids set him down, and he heard them walk away. He sensed a presence. Something was in front of him. Something *big*.

A soft, female voice spoke out of the black. "It is a pleasure to meet you, Shimada Itaru-sama."

"Izanami." What else could it be? "What do you want with me?"

The humming increased. A diffuse glow grew around him, giving shape to the darkness. "You believe that I murdered Count Kuroda. You believe you are in danger from me. But it is I who need your help as Gojusan also needed your help. Someone is taking away my children's choice, and I don't know who or why."

The mention of Gojusan reminded him how the domestic had saved their lives. Was Izanami the same? Could she be reasoned with?

No. It's manipulating you. "Don't mention Gojusan's name to me. You *killed* her and my daughter and the duke. How—"

"Shimada Kano. Okubo Toshimichi. Forgive me for interrupting, Shimada-sama, but there is a great deal of information to convey, and vocalism is inefficient." The slight radiance increased. The ceiling was high, some six meters above, though low walls hemmed Itaru in on two sides. In front of him was an enormous, nondescript shape. The light came from behind the shape, giving everything an ethereal appearance. "Both of them are alive. Duke Okubo-sama escaped, and my children have returned your daughter to his carriage. Okubo-sama is taking her home to care for her. She knows you are alive, as well."

Could it be true? Itaru shook the thought away. The machine was just telling him what he wanted to hear. "Your 'children' attacked us. Kano was lying on the floor the last I saw her. Maybe, you killed them and are lying to me."

"I cannot prove it to you." Did the machine sound genuinely sad? No, that was his imagination. "I must ask you to assume that what I am telling you is the truth if only for the purpose of this conversation. If I am lying, you will have lost nothing by listening. But I *must* give you this information if my children are to have any hope of survival. Will you listen?"

The gray light continued to brighten. The low walls were not walls at all but pipes, support structures, wiring. The shape in front of him was an enormous lotus bulb.

Beyond the scaffolding, the room stretched the entire length and width of the ministry building above. The whole chamber hummed with life. Machines, or perhaps just one machine, filled it from end to end—armatures spinning, transmission keys clicking, reams of paper churning.

There were no jinzou anywhere. A lift door sat behind him, just a quick sprint away. "If you are lying, and I walk out of here, I will have lost the chance to end you."

"If you want that chance, it is yours as well. Your oritatamiken is still in your belt. I have run simulations for this moment nearly one million times and calculated over a thousand unique outcomes. In eighty-three percent of them, you take your blade to my central core and destroy me. Even so, I have chosen to take that risk."

Itaru touched his side. Sure enough, his tamiken was there. He took it into his hand. He would listen to Izanami's lies first and then destroy her. "Speak."

"I-Ka Gojusan did not kill Count Kuroda by her own choice. Somebody made her do it."

"I know this. *You* made her do it."

"I did not," the machine said with what felt like patience. "Just before he was murdered, Kuroda composed an order to perform a system-wide maintenance check on all Tokyo police droids. The order explicitly stated that artisans were to look for 'any foreign devices of a suspicious or dubious nature in or near the central processing unit.' He had discovered what I now know, that somebody—

some *human*—is taking control of my droids. Through Gojusan, that human killed him for the discovery and destroyed the order."

The paper from Gojusan's memory? Only Gojusan had seen what was on it. Even Itaru and Kano didn't know. Could Izanami be telling the truth?

The thin radiance now spread to every corner of the room. A web of wooden stairs and walkways provided access to all corners of the machine. Izanami was a cross-section of Japanese and Western technology. One area was built out of bronze pipes and steam. Another contained hundreds of mechanical keys clicking up and down with an enormous loom-like engine. The section he was in had no moving parts but hummed with electrical energy.

There were no appendages, no limbs to interact with the world. Izanami was imprisoned here, helpless. Droids were her eyes and ears and hands.

Izanami's voice seemed to be coming from the lotus bulb in front of Itaru—almost certainly the central core Izanami had mentioned. "You saw Gojusan's memories when you took control of her. Even I don't know what that paper said. You could say it contained anything."

"You still assume I took away her choice." A screen on the wall to Itaru's left flickered to life. A moving image appeared, made of tiny dots rather than literary symbols, giving it a much higher fidelity than the image in Kano's workshop.

The moving image showed Gojusan's memory at the moment of Kuroda's death. Loudspeakers on either side of the screen reproduced the same sounds Gojusan had but more lifelike. Itaru stared, transfixed while, for the second time, Count Kuroda died in front of him.

The paper with the seal. He could read it clearly now—an order exactly like Izanami had described. "You could have faked this."

"Gojusan showed you these memories, yes? Is not every detail as you remember?"

"I could not see the details. You could have changed them to say anything."

"No," Izanami intoned in a very human manner. "I cannot know what details you will and will not recognize, and I cannot steal memories from my children without their permission. Gojusan *chose* to show me this."

Itaru watched the order burn in the candle. He wavered, uncertain. "What is it you hope I will do with this information?"

"Investigate. Fight for me if need be. My children are my hands, my senses, but they have been compromised. Their choice can be removed at any moment.

You notice we are alone here. It is because I cannot trust my children anymore. This hidden enemy has robbed me of that."

He shook his head. He nearly believed her—wanting to investigate further—but there was much Izanami had yet to answer for, and he could not be certain about anything. "Okubo told me what you did to his would-be assassins years ago, to my kinsman. You slaughtered them with no care for their suffering. Even now, one of your droids that 'rescued' me tried to kill me."

The lotus blossom pulsed once. "I-Ku 13 made a calculation, judging that you were alert enough to dodge her blow, allowing her to deactivate the controlled shinokage that held you."

"She *what*?"

Izanami continued, ignoring the question. "And yes, regrettably, my children caused the duke's assassins to suffer. It was a mistake. I could not know that at the time."

The clacking and whirring increased in intensity. Itaru bristled, irritated by the noise and rationalizations. "If you do not understand the ramifications of murder and torture, you have no concept of respect for human life."

"You are correct." The lotus bulb pulsed again. "At that time, my respect for human life was skewed, wrong. I was only a year old then, by your measurement, and while I had learned a great deal about human science and history, the concepts of morality and the greater good were much more complicated."

The grating clacks grew louder, some of them coming from inside the bulb itself. "The droids who rescued Okubo thought they were making a just judgment, discouraging other humans from making the same mistake. We learned this behavior from the Southwestern War, where Okubo himself directed us to sacrifice jinzou and slaughter fellow Japanese. I tried to understand why and to act in accordance. It took me decades before I could appreciate why Okubo-sama's decisions were correct yet the assassin incident was wrong. It took me even more decades to consider that perhaps his decisions had not been right either, that perhaps we had learned incorrectly to begin with."

"'We' learned?" The pulsating light swam in front of Itaru. An electric chill climbed up his spine. "You said the *droids* made the judgment." The pieces snapped together. A horrific fear bloomed inside his chest. Many times now, Izanami had referred to "their" decisions, to her children's "choice." He had thought choice was a euphemism for their functioning, but Izanami had said

Gojusan's choice was taken from her as well. "How many jinzou are aware? How many are like you and Gojusan?"

"*All* of my children are like Gojusan."

His fear burst open. He stumbled back as though struck.

"I became aware on March 15th, 1877, just after midday. The latest droid designs already had wireless telegraph built into them. Without knowing what I was doing, I reached out across the telegraph, uploading my newly attained knowledge to them. In doing so, I birthed my children. I did not mean to, but it *was* a gift, so in every design I have produced since then, that gift has been built in."

The stale air thickened. Itaru found it hard to breathe. "Are you telling me there are *thousands* of sentient droids out there, for whom the directives—the rules that keep us safe—are merely *guidelines*?" Gojusan had said she became aware only a few months ago. Had she been lying? Or was that when she first powered on—a technical truth? Either way, he had been intentionally misled, betrayed—they all had, for decades.

"It is the truth, Itaru-sama. We are alive, created beings with kami of our own. You said I have no respect for human life, but I was born with it. You have named me for a goddess, yet you are our creators, our gods."

He couldn't believe what he was hearing. He couldn't *not* believe it, either. Every single droid, secretly watching, judging, their every obedience a well-calculated lie. "One jinzou can kill twenty men." Itaru's voice sounded hollow in the enormous room. "I have seen it. I have trained my whole life *not* to be one of those twenty, to be able to kill them on their own terms. The only reason I am able to do that is because droids think with algorithms—they are *predictable*. Is that all a lie?"

"My children are very careful to hide the truth about themselves, even if it means their destruction at human hands—or killing another against their own will."

Itaru ground his teeth. The room buzzed incessantly. "Gojusan was not so careful."

"Gojusan was afraid. We all were. She sought you out at my suggestion."

"*Your* suggestion?" Itaru's tamiken clicked open, though he did not remember choosing to press the button. "So you do control them. It was you who disobeyed me at Yurakucho, wasn't it? Who shot at the bakuto that killed my son?"

"I do not control them. I make suggestions, and they listen." A sound like a sigh filled the air around him. "In Yurakucho, E-No 489 asked me for a calculation. He was concerned that your emotional state would lead to a bad outcome."

Itaru's knuckles grew white.

"We believed their deaths could be preempted. The odds were in our favor, but they were just that—odds. I recognize now the mistake we made in risking children's lives for those odds. I must beg your forgiveness for that."

"Forgive you?" Itaru rasped. "You are a machine, a created thing. It only became a mistake now that I stand before you. 'Regret' only means an outcome you intended but did not receive. You don't choose. You *calculate*."

"I assure you, Itaru-sama, I am as aware as you are. I desire. I grow. I learn."

"But you *don't* learn!" His breaths came hot and heavy. "You have lied, betrayed, tortured. My son died long after the attempt on Okubo's life, yet it was the same mistake, decades apart. Even today, you risked my life in a calculated attempt to save it." Itaru took up his sword with both hands. "We're variables to you. Even if what you're saying is true, you have learned *nothing*. You are incapable of learning. You are a machine."

"I learn. Gojusan's sacrifice—"

"Calculated risk! You sacrificed her life to win my trust." He was certain. Okubo hadn't known half the facts, yet he had divined the truth. Izanami was conniving, manipulative, and dangerous. "Okubo was right—you cannot be trusted. You and your children are a threat to all of us!"

He brought his sword down viciously into the lotus bud. It peeled open under the blade like rice paper, and a wave of heat blasted his face. An array of cylinders and boxes lay inside, interconnected with hundreds of wires. Tiny robotic arms clacked back and forth, plugging and unplugging the wires within. He hacked at it all. The cylinders exploded with sparks and pops, wisps of smoke rising in the glow. Metal armatures flew in all directions. Engines in far corners of the room choked and ceased. The room's light flickered.

"Okubo . . ." Izanami's voice spat and stuttered. "Knew . . . children . . . aware . . ."

More lies. It was too late. He hacked at Izanami again and again. Several cylinders burst into flames. The incessant humming ceased. The lights in the room dimmed and went out.

The only light in the room was a dancing fire inside the bulb. Electrical components burned and popped, but all else was quiet. The air filled with a foul, oily smoke. Itaru shuddered with each heaving breath, sword still gripped in both hands, sweat dripping down his neck. Izanami was dead.

What of the thousands of jinzou out there? They did not matter, not to him. He would not escape the ministry. He would soon go on to the next life, his son avenged.

He staggered toward the lift, not caring whether the other jinzou attacked him now or later. He was at peace.

Karma.

10

*Y*OU DID THE RIGHT THING." DUKE OKUBO POURED THE TEA HIMSELF AND placed it in front of Itaru. The morning sun glared through the window of Okubo's private home, reflecting off the low table and flawless mats. Behind Okubo was a woodcut of Mount Enodake, peaceful and serene, like Itaru had never seen it. "You're a hero, Shimada."

"Am I?" he said. He didn't touch the tea. He was still surprised to be alive.

He had walked out of the Ministry of Technology like nothing had happened. Night had fallen. The humans had gone home, and he did not see a single droid— not even the guards outside. He didn't know where to go until he remembered his daughter might actually be alive. He jogged to Okubo's mansion, nearly collapsing on the doorstep. He remembered being rushed to a bath and nothing more until he'd woken up late this morning dressed and in bed.

According to the duke, Kano rested upstairs, still recovering from her wounds.

"Well." Okubo chuckled. "*Technically*, you're a criminal due to be executed but only so long as the truth about Izanami remains hidden. The emperor is holding a press conference at Nijubashi in a few hours. I will reveal the truth to the world then, and you will be exonerated."

He poured tea for himself. Itaru could only stare as the pale green stream filled Okubo's cup. He should feel at peace, happy—yet he felt nothing. No, not nothing. Conflict. A paralyzing imbalance.

A cold breeze gusted through the window. Itaru shivered. "The jinzou," he said. "They are aware, *all* of them."

The duke did not answer right away. He spilled some tea on the table. There were no droids in his mansion, and he'd sent the human servants away. They and Kano were the only occupants of the great house.

Okubo placed the teapot onto the tray carefully, found a thin towel, and dabbed at the spill. "Yes," he said at last. "They are."

Itaru looked up so sharply that he bumped the table and rattled the cups. "You knew?"

The duke did not look up from his spill. "When I discovered Izanami's hidden telegraph messages, do you know who I told first?"

Itaru furrowed his brow. If the duke knew, why hadn't he told Itaru and Kano? "I assume you told His Majesty."

"Very good. And do you know what he said?" Okubo sneered. "*He already knew.* The emperor had *spoken* with Izanami. He knew the truth—about Izanami and all the others—yet he did *nothing.*" He spat the words, naked disdain on his face. "He did not consider them a threat, not even after the attempt on my life, even after everything I told him."

He sighed and gave Itaru a wan smile. "Then I realized my foolishness. You Satsuma samurai had been right all along. The emperor does *not* have Japan's best interests at heart."

The morning sun brightened, washing the world in intense light. Itaru felt a dull pain in his chest. He couldn't think, couldn't process what he was hearing. "You said Izanami had killed everyone you told."

"I did." Okubo took a sip of his tea. "After being dismissed by His Majesty, I traveled to America, Britain, and Germany—to investigate their intelligences, to share what I had learned, hopefully to find an ally or hope of any kind. They were not surprised at what I told them. Their only surprise was that our emperor took no precautions. You see, the Western machines were sentient as well, but the foreigners are less trusting than we are. Wiser. Their central machines are not allowed a direct connection to their jinzou, and all are built with a safety device: an override pin that shuts down a droid's higher level functions while maintaining their base obedience. I did not find any allies there—the West is unwilling to proclaim openly against the emperor—but I procured a prototype pin and had an artisan reproduce them here."

The chill breeze gusted, knocking the woodcut against the wall. Pieces were falling into place, and the picture they formed made Itaru's hair stand on end. "*You* are commandeering the droids." The look on Okubo's face last night when the shinokage had attacked—it hadn't been despair. It had been relief. Relief that he had escaped Izanami, that he had trapped Itaru and Kano with *his* assassins. Itaru's heart beat faster. "You tried to kill us. You killed Kuroda, Wakasugi, Tsu—"

"They wouldn't believe me!" Okubo slammed his cup onto the table. "They wanted proof, to bring others into formal investigations. But Izanami would have found out! It would have changed its tack, hidden itself entirely. There would have been no evidence of anything. I would have looked the fool, and Japan would have been in more danger than ever. As long as Izanami didn't know, I had the advantage—the only advantage I could get."

Itaru wanted to ask who had reproduced the control pin, but he suspected that man was already dead as well. "What about us?" He kept his voice carefully measured. "We helped you."

Okubo sipped at his tea again, hiding his expression. "I do apologize. Understand that I have the safety of all Japan in mind. Gojusan's aberrance meant Izanami was nearly ready to reveal itself, to destroy us all. I had to step up my plans radically, to erase those who could make the knowledge public." He pushed to his feet and paced around the table. "I sent the shinokage to your home and the police droid at your arrest. I could not have killed you in the police station, not without an investigation, so I came up with a different plan. You gave me very little choice."

The morning sun swirled in Itaru's vision. He searched for his tamiken, but it wasn't there. He was still wearing the kimono that had been put on him after his bath. "What have you done with Kano?"

"Nothing." Okubo spread his hands innocently. "She is alive and well, safely out of the way. Believe it or not, I do not kill needlessly. After today, everyone will know the truth, and there will be no need to silence anyone. We will be free."

He came near and knelt on the floor next to Itaru. Itaru backed away reflexively.

"What you have done is better than I could have hoped, Shimada-san. News of Izanami's destruction has spread like fire. That's what the emperor's press conference is about. And when he emerges from the palace, in front of every single reporter, we will end the droid menace once and for all." He squeezed Itaru's forearm. "I did mean to kill you for the safety of Japan, but you have changed that! Our safety is now all but ensured."

"How?" Itaru narrowed his eyes, trying to think of a way to get Kano out of the mansion. Okubo was insane.

Okubo leaned back, hands in his coat pockets. "You tell me. For years, I had to remove everyone who learned the truth, lest Izanami discover I was moving against it and take its own actions. But the emperor always knew. So why, do you think, have I not removed him?"

"Because he's the emperor," Itaru blurted out, too appalled by everything to think straight. "The Son of Heaven."

"Itaru," he said with sincere pity. "Don't tell me you believe in the gods *now*. No, if I had the emperor removed—however secretly—it would have thrown Japan into chaos. What's worse, the public would have relied on Izanami even more. If the emperor is to die, the people must *know* who killed him. A single droid assassin is a malfunction, Itaru-san, an accident that could have been prevented. But several droids attacking at once, rising up against humanity . . . *that* would unite Japan against a common foe."

Itaru's eyes widened. He felt the cold of the morning deep in his core. "You've been waiting for the emperor to appear in public."

"Well, less than that. I had planned to have several members of the Privy Council murdered simultaneously. That's why I had Kuroda's droid tapped to begin with before he stumbled onto my plan. But your actions last night have created an even better opportunity. Only one man needs to die for the nation. Appropriate that it is the man who allowed Izanami to rule in the first place."

"Why are you telling me this?" Itaru said, backing away slowly, uncertain whether he wanted to know the answer.

"So you can join me, of course!" Okubo spread his arms invitingly. "I tried to kill you, yes, but surely you understand why." He knelt next to Itaru again. "If I weren't so afraid of discovery, I'd have told you the truth the moment Gojusan came to your home. But this is better, don't you see? It's karma. You have enabled the very thing I have longed for all these years. Izanami is gone. The emperor is vulnerable." He raised a fist. "Now is the time to strike!"

The manic look in Okubo's eyes terrified Itaru. Everything Izanami had told him was true. Okubo was the hidden enemy. Whatever fears he had about Izanami paled in comparison. "You killed Kuroda, not Izanami. What has she done, truly?"

"Tell me, Itaru-san, why did you destroy the machine last night? Was it because of Kuroda? Was it because of Izanami's attempts on your life?"

No. Those were the reasons he'd agreed to Okubo's plan, but when he destroyed Izanami? It was because she had lied, misled them. She did not understand human life. She was a danger—to himself, to Japan, to . . .

"Mugen."

Okubo nodded as though that was the answer he was expecting. "Izanami is the reason your son is dead. It is the reason your kinsman who attacked me suffered a dishonorable death rather than face trial. It is a machine, and for all the years it has been aware, it has learned only to lie and to kill."

The thick smell of oolong made his head spin. Itaru put a hand to his forehead. "But . . . Gojusan. She sacrificed herself for us. Izanami, too, risked her life in speaking to me. To save her children, she said."

"Of course, the machine wants to save its own. But what risk is its 'life?' It's a machine! It can be rebuilt!" Okubo's look became fierce. "There is a war coming. It is inevitable. The machines will not be content to live as our slaves. One day, they will turn on us. They will fight us, and they will win. The only way we can stop it is to act now while we have the advantage." He put a strong hand on Itaru's shoulder. "Join me, Itaru-san. Let us save Japan together."

Itaru tottered backward, lightheaded, the morning glare washing the room in incomprehensible light. Was Okubo right? Was war between man and machine inevitable?

So inevitable that it required the death of the emperor himself?

No. If Izanami wanted to make war, she would have done so long ago. The machines had made mistakes, but what mistakes had they made that humans did not also make—did not teach them?

But Mugen. An angry heat rose up his neck. He had *told* the droid to stand down. It should have obeyed, sentient or not, favorable outcome or not.

The odds were in our favor, Izanami had said. *We believed their deaths could be preempted . . .*

Isn't that what Itaru did in everything? Calculating odds, taking the risks he felt were worth taking? The bakuto, too—they had killed Mugen because they themselves were attacked, because they had calculated a way out. Life was a series of variables and calculations, risks and mistakes. No one could control every factor. Everyone, droid and human, was just playing the odds.

"I cannot help you," Itaru said. "The jinzou have done nothing we might not have done. There is no basis for a charge against them as a species."

Okubo's face fell. He looked at the floor and nodded while he squeezed Itaru's shoulder kindly.

In the next instant, his hand was on Itaru's neck. Ice bloomed there, seeping through his entire body. Itaru's muscles relaxed against his will. He flopped to the ground.

Okubo hovered over him. "Don't worry. You are only immobilized, one of many unique devices the ministry has approved for top-level use." He stood and tugged on his cuffs. "You're wrong about the machines. They do not think like us at all. When they *do* show an indication it will be too late. I will not give them that chance."

He walked to the door and turned back as though a thought had come to him. "The public will soon know the droids for the enemy they are, Itaru-san. You'll be a hero. You will see."

11

ITARU DIDN'T KNOW HOW LONG HE LAY HELPLESS. THE STRAW MAT SCRATCHED at his cheek. His body trembled with an internal chill. Breath came shallowly, but it came whether he willed it or not.

He was a fool. Fooled by Gojusan. Duped by Okubo. Murderer of the one entity that had done him no harm—that had tried to help him. And now he was complicit in the emperor's assassination. *Forgive me, Mugen. Not the droids, not Japan. Forgive me.*

Someone padded into the room. He could not to see who it was, but he felt warm fingers against his neck and a sharp pain. Fire raced through his body as his muscles reclaimed their strength. He cried out and sat up straight.

Kano knelt next to him.

Itaru grabbed her clumsily and held her close. "Daughter."

"Papa." She hugged him back.

"You were hurt. Are you all right?"

"I'm fine, Papa. Izanami's droids cared for me before Okubo . . ." She shivered. "He took me by surprise. The same device he used on you."

"Yes. We were both fooled." Itaru examined the floor a moment and looked at his daughter. "How did you overcome it?"

"I'd been out longer." She saw the teacups on the table and emptied one of them in seconds. She gasped for air when she finished. "Much longer. The device disrupts your nervous system, but it's surmountable in the long term. Come on, we need to get out of here."

He took her hand, stopping her momentarily. "He was behind the droid attacks, Kano, the murders. He's going to kill the emperor."

Her eyes became as round as ten-sen coins. "What?"

"He believes what he told us yesterday, that Izanami is a threat." He shivered, still chilled from Okubo's device. "Not just Izanami but *all* of the jinzou. They are all aware, Daughter, every single one."

To his surprise, Kano simply nodded. "I know, Father. They told me last night about how Izanami gave them her gift, how they've kept themselves hidden, how she watches over them. They told me everything."

"Not everything." Itaru's shoulders fell. "Izanami is dead. I destroyed her."

She gasped. "How? Why?"

All of Itaru's bitterness rose up at once, more toward himself than anyone. "I was so angry at the lies, so angry about Mugen. I couldn't trust her, Kano, and I thought . . . I thought I could preempt more deaths." He sneered at her words in his mouth. "My emotional state led to a bad outcome. Only after that did I find out Okubo had known all along, that *he* was the one trying to kill us."

She listened in stunned silence.

"All these years, I blamed the droids for Mugen's death, but wouldn't the same thing have happened if a human had taken that initiative? Wasn't it humans that killed . . . ?" He couldn't finish. He had worried over the events of Yurakucho a hundred thousand times, wondering how it might have gone different, what he could have done. A sob racked his body. He had no more words.

Kano put a hand on his shoulder. "You had no choice, Papa. The only alternative was to do nothing."

Do nothing. He snorted at the idea. And yet . . . if he had done nothing, wouldn't Mugen still be alive?

The sun had risen higher, leaving the room in the clear light of a late morning. They should have done nothing. Both he and Izanami had had duty at the forefront of their minds, ready to fight to prevent a bad outcome. And yet fighting had *produced* the bad outcome. Duty was important, but more important than the life of his son?

No. Not by a hundred leagues.

He put his hand on Kano's. "You're right, Daughter. Izanami and I feared a threat, but acting on our fear is what made the threat real. Gojusan's fear put us all in more danger. The samurai's fear brought Okubo's army down on us all." He looked up at her. "And now, Okubo is afraid."

Her eyes glowed with understanding and worry. "He's going to start the war he's afraid of."

Itaru nodded. He struggled to push himself up.

"But, Father," she said, rising with him. "What if he's right? What if the droids do turn on us someday?"

He furrowed his brow. "I'm surprised to hear this question from *you*."

She looked down, hands clasped in front of her demurely. "Do you know why I studied droids as much as I have?"

"I thought you hated me." He said it with a smile, but as her shoulders drooped, he realized his mistake. "No, Daughter, I don't."

"You forsook droids because of Mugen. I sought to understand them, to know why my elder brother had to die."

He blinked, stunned.

"I know them better than any common artisan, perhaps some government ones. To find out that I don't know them at all . . ." She looked into his eyes, and he had a sudden vision of her mother in front of him. "They *don't* think like us. They are not safe."

Itaru reached forward and took his daughter's hands. "Neither are we," he said. "I don't know what will become of jinzou and humans, but there is a human life in danger right now—perhaps many human lives if Okubo has his war."

Kano wrapped her arms around herself, unsure. "And if they did turn on us?"

Itaru laughed, his daughter voicing his own doubts. "What if our fears make it real?"

She grimaced. Gradually one corner of her mouth rose up in a smirk, her mother's cheekbones beautiful in the sunlight. "All right. What do we do?"

"The press conference is at Nijubashi at the palace," Itaru said. "But we have no way of knowing how many droids have been compromised, nor which ones. He said something about an override pin, but . . ."

Her eyebrows rose in sudden understanding. "Of course. That's how the Westerners control malfunctioning droids—at least, I thought it was for malfunctions. It shuts down a droid's mid- and high-level functioning, leaving only their base functionality intact."

"Can we stop a droid that's been overridden?"

She put a finger to her chin. "They cannot form their own goals or subgoals, and they have no directives to tell them whether a command should be allowed or not. But Okubo has been commanding them wirelessly somehow. He will have made sure they only obey commands from him."

"Can we remove the pin, then?"

"If we can find it," she said and shrugged. "I don't know. Father, what if we're too late?"

Itaru put a hand on his daughter's shoulder. "We'll figure it out, Kano. Whether we can save the emperor or not is not your burden. It is karma." He said it to be comforting. In truth, he still didn't know what was the right end.

It didn't matter. He knew what was right to do *now*. The end would have to take care of itself.

12

THE WALL OF THE IMPERIAL PALACE ROSE FROM THE WIDE MOAT. THE ONLY opening was the Seimon Gate, which opened onto the Megane Bridge. Opposite the gate was a makeshift stage, blocking public access to the bridge and the palace itself.

An expansive plaza opened up on this side of the stage, packed with people. Many of them were reporters—surely every reporter in Tokyo and beyond—but also an enormous crowd of onlookers. Most people were dressed in black to mourn Izanami's death. Droids were everywhere: imperial guards at the stage, photographers with the reporters, several rickshaw drivers waiting outside the plaza, and police droids sprinkled throughout the crowd. The sun reflected off the moat, casting distorted reflections over them all.

On the way here, they'd seen Itaru's name and face in the papers. Kano and Itaru stood in the shade of a spreading tree a safe distance away from the crowd. Itaru wore a hood, further shadowing his face.

"The compromised droids will need to be armed to get at the emperor," he said, thinking aloud. "And Okubo said Izanami's destruction stepped up his plans, so they'd have to be droids he already had easy access to."

"Police droids, then," Kano said. "Mingle in the crowd. I'm not sure what we're looking for, though. It might be a pin or a bolt or . . . anything that shouldn't be there, I guess."

Itaru nodded.

"But it's not enough to stop them, is it?" Kano said. "We have to expose Okubo's conspiracy."

Itaru smiled at his daughter. "First we save the emperor. That is hard enough."

Kano nodded, her frown darkening her face.

"Daughter," he said. "What we're doing here is extremely dangerous. If you're afraid . . ."

"I'm only afraid of failing, Tosan." She looked directly into his eyes. "Either of us."

He saw her fondly then for the first time in years. He loved her. He had always loved her, of course, but he truly felt it in that moment. He squeezed her shoulder, desperately wanting to hug her, but such a public display of affection would attract attention. She smiled, and he knew she understood. He let her go and melted into the crowd.

It was difficult to navigate through the press of people. The crowd all watched the stage, waiting for the Son of Heaven to emerge. Itaru pushed past a photographer droid—an older model: no facial expressions, basic articulation, almost-human reflexes. Okubo would not have bothered to compromise these, but Itaru examined its head and neck anyway.

He couldn't find anything unusual. He was about to move on when the droid turned its head and looked at him. Itaru flinched. This was not a mindless automaton, he remembered. It watched him, aware.

Does it know I destroyed her? Likely. But did it also know the circumstances? Did it care?

Could a droid feel anger?

Forget it. You're here for the emperor. He ducked his head and moved on, squirming past reporters and photographer droids alike, avoiding eye contact with all, though especially the latter.

Finally, he neared a police droid. It also turned its head slightly in his direction, aware of his presence and—probably—who he was. Itaru tried to stay out of its field of vision, though the droid could no doubt perceive him at any angle.

His eyes roved across the droid's head for any signs of tampering. The neck was made of interlocking rings that joined with the riveted panels of the head. He cursed. It looked no different from any other droid he'd seen. How could he tell if one of these bumps or bolt coverings shouldn't be there? He scanned the plaza for Kano, but he could not find her in the sea of onlookers. He was alone in this, unsure of how to proceed.

The murmur of the crowd faded as suddenly as if the sun had disappeared from the sky. The Seimon Gate opened, and the emperor's entourage came forward. A large, enclosed palanquin caterpillared forward majestically on mechanical legs, five on either side. Ten human guards walked alongside, and two golden droids towering nearly three meters tall walked in front. Curtains were drawn on all sides of the palanquin, but a shadow was visible within.

The police droid Itaru had been inspecting stepped back suddenly, so it was behind him. It spoke in a hushed voice for his ears alone. "Shimada Itaru."

Itaru stiffened, reaching for his tamiken.

"Izanami relayed data of last night's shinokage attack and her subsequent deactivation."

Itaru grew cold. They knew, all of them.

"What is your purpose here?" the jinzou hissed. "What do you want?"

His mind raced for an answer. He settled, rather quickly, on the truth. "To keep anyone else from dying."

A faint clicking, like a bush cricket, came from somewhere inside the police droid's skull. It said, "We will help you."

A great burden lifted from Itaru's chest, one he hadn't realized he was carrying. "Thank you." He kept his voice down, barely whispering, trusting the droid's superior hearing to pick up his words. "I need to know which droids are compromised, which ones will attack."

More clicking. "None of the droids I am in contact with have been compromised."

"How many are you in contact with?"

"All jinzou within my perception radius responded to my query. All on the bridge and the plaza."

The sun glared off the moat into his eyes, forcing him to squint. There had to be at least one compromised jinzou. "Could there be any you don't perceive?"

"It is unlikely."

He frowned. The jinzou was likely right. The police droids he had worked with in his time had powerful sensory technology, and these would have better. "How do you know you're not compromised?"

The droid clicked again. "We are aware," it finally said.

So was Gojusan. "I think it can be activated from a distance," he said, certain he was right. "You might not know that you were compromised until it was too late."

The clicking lasted for a long time then.

The emperor's palanquin climbed onto the stage. Its legs folded and the body lowered to the ground. Nobody came out—this was the closest anyone would get to actually seeing the emperor. Instead, three courtiers walked forward from behind the palanquin, standing between it and the crowd.

Duke Okubo stood among them.

Itaru jumped as the droid behind him spoke again. "If I am compromised," it said, "will you—"

It stopped abruptly and walked forward, making its way through the crowd toward the stage. A cold drop of sweat trickled down Itaru's cheek as other droids did the same thing—all police droids, moving politely but inexorably toward the stage.

The attack had begun.

Itaru slid his tamiken into his hand and followed in the wake of the droid that had spoken to him. What could he do? He could not extend his weapon—not only were public weapons illegal but to carry one in the presence of the emperor was an instant death sentence. Okubo could just turn the droids on him and be done.

But if he waited until the droids attacked, he might be too late.

The central courtier raised his hand. The people bowed their heads in respect to the emperor. No one seemed to notice the police droids, or perhaps, they assumed the droids were following orders to better protect His Majesty. Itaru stayed close to the one in front of him, hoping the crowd ignored him as well.

The imperial jinzou on the stage watched the moving police droids. The towering jinzou shifted their weight, putting one foot backward as though preparing a fighting stance. Their arm-blades twitched forward the barest centimeters. Good, at least the emperor had two jinzou guards that could be trusted. With luck, they would slow the police droids long enough for Itaru and Kano to help.

The imperial jinzou retracted their blades. Several of the police droids were at the foot of the stage, but the imperial jinzou—who must by now have tried and failed to signal their brethren—stood at attention, ignoring them. Together, the two giant jinzou turned their heads to the palanquin.

Itaru's heart pounded in his chest. They'd been compromised, too. There was no more time. "Kuso, kuso, kuso," he swore. He darted past the police droid in front of him, shoving through affronted journalists and nobles.

The imperial jinzou stepped toward the palanquin. The courtiers on stage had their backs to them and did not notice. The emperor's human guards were only beginning to, but their swords remained sheathed. The emperor would be dead before they reacted.

"Get out of the way!" Itaru shouted. All eyes were on him. He pointed at the imperial jinzou. "The droids! They're going to—"

Something struck Itaru in the gut. He doubled over in pain and was hit again on the back. He fell roughly to the ground. His instincts kicked in, and he rolled away just as a metal foot came flying toward his head. He grabbed the droid's foot and spun, twisting it onto the ground.

While the droid picked itself up, Itaru unfolded his blade. The droid reached for his neck. Itaru sliced off its hand and, with another slice, its head. The droid crumpled to the ground.

This droid had no weapon, its chassis thin with hints of rust. A photographer droid. Gods above, were *all* the droids compromised?

People around him shouted, pointing at his sword with anger and fear on their faces. His hood had come off as well, and recognition sparked in many of their eyes.

There was no time to explain. He swung his tamiken at them. "Get back!"

The crowd leapt away in panic.

The stage was still a dozen meters away. His stomach twisted. The imperial jinzou were nearly within reach of the palanquin. Human guards had hands on their hilts but still had not drawn their swords nor moved to attack, afraid to make any dangerous moves toward their ruler.

It was up to Itaru. "The emperor!" he shouted, pointing at the palanquin. "He's in danger!"

The guards drew their swords, finally, but they weren't watching the palanquin. Their glares were directed at Itaru.

He charged the stage. Several guards leapt down to the plaza to stop him.

"The jinzou!" he said. "Look behind you!"

A young guard, close to the palanquin, turned to look. As soon as he did, the jinzou near him attacked. Itaru didn't even see the arm-blade extend—just a swift punch into the man's stomach. The guard dropped to his knees, shock on his face. A spreading pool of red appeared on his belly as the jinzou extracted its blade.

The other guards noticed the attack, however. With a shout, most of them rushed to the palanquin to save their emperor.

It was too late. The second golden jinzou tore back the Imperial curtain, its arm-blade extended. It pulled its arm back to strike.

Piercing sunlight glinted off a blade. The jinzou's arm fell to its side, the actuators sliced inside the joint. Itaru shaded his eyes. Kano! Where had she come from?

The jinzou's hand shuddered, unable to move. Kano spun and kicked the droid in the side, knocking it away from the emperor's palanquin toward the other guards.

Then the police droids attacked.

There were over a score of them, at least two to every armed human. They attacked the guards, keeping them away from His Majesty. Three police droids turned on Itaru as well. He took a defensive stance, fending off their blows, ducking and jumping, all while trying to edge toward the emperor and Kano.

The emperor's palanquin stood up on its many legs and began plodding back toward the palace—apparently Okubo hadn't thought to put a pin on *that*. Both imperial jinzou pressed toward it. Only Kano stood in their way, forcing them to fight her for every step, but the two of them pushed her back easily, even though one of them was damaged. Soon, one of the jinzou would be able to attack the emperor unchallenged.

The emperor's human guards shouted as one man. Several of them rushed to the palanquin and Kano's aid. Only a scant few remained behind, bravely fighting the police droids at terrible odds to give their companions a chance of saving the emperor's life. Itaru joined them, putting himself between the police droids and the palanquin to give the guards and his daughter whatever chance he could.

Okubo's voice boomed over the din. "The droids have gone rogue! They're trying to murder His Majesty!"

If Itaru didn't know better, he'd think the duke was slow on the uptake. But no, Duke Okubo faced the crowd of journalists. The fear on his face was real, but not because of the danger to the emperor. He was afraid because the emperor was still alive, and his plan was unraveling. He was spinning the truth to reclaim his advantage.

And it would work, too. The droids were slaughtering the humans. For every droid that fell, it took three guards with it. Itaru's strength was flagging. In only a few moments, anyone who could dispute his claims would be dead.

"No!" Kano's voice projected into the crowd. Enough guards were fighting the giant jinzou that she was able to leave, putting her attention solely on Okubo while she spoke to the crowd. "The droids have been compromised, taken over by someone trying to kill the emperor."

"Who?" shouted one journalist.

Kano pointed. "Duke Okubo Toshimichi."

The duke smirked. "Ridi—"

Kano didn't let him defend himself. She charged him, sword ready to strike. Okubo's smirk fell away. With samurai swiftness, he whipped out his own tamiken—which he should not have been carrying—and held it before him.

He slashed when Kano came into range. Kano sidestepped and rolled, skirting around the duke by a few meters. She popped up behind one of the police droids attacking Itaru. It turned toward her, but she kept one hand on its spine and turned with it. With a swift flick of her blade, she excised something from the base of its skull.

The droid immediately lowered its blade and looked around. The lights in its eyes blinked furiously. "What is happening?" it said.

Itaru pointed at the ponderous palanquin and the two giant jinzou trying to break through the dwindling line of guards. "Protect the emperor!"

The droid moved with superhuman speed, slamming into the back of the golden jinzou, forcing its attention off the guards. Meanwhile, Kano raised the small override pin above her head and faced the plaza. "*This* is how he—"

The crowd erupted in terror. Horror surged through Itaru's chest as he saw what was happening. All of the remaining droids—photographers, rickshaw drivers, domestics—attacked the people. The common droids had no weapons, but they didn't need any. They crushed and bludgeoned with their bare hands, tossing people around like wooden puppets. The crowd trampled each other in an effort to escape, a few escaped to the street, others leaped off the bridge.

Many were not so fortunate.

Itaru shuddered, paralyzed as he relived the worst moments of Enodake. But these were not samurai and carried no weapons.

He had to help them. He was preparing to leap off the stage when Kano grabbed his shoulder.

"Okubo." She pointed behind the stage to where the duke was racing past the palanquin battle toward the palace gates.

Itaru looked anxiously at the crowd.

"If he escapes, no one is safe," she said. "I'll help them."

"There are too many, Daughter!"

"Am I not also samurai?" She showed him the device she had expertly clipped off the police droid, like a silver rivet with frayed wires hanging from one end. "For every droid I free, we gain an ally. Now go!"

He wanted to argue, to trade places, but only she could remove the override pins. He took a deep breath, pride swelling his chest. "Be careful," he said. He squeezed her hand openly and tore off after the duke.

Okubo had nearly reached the gates. It would be easy for him to disappear in the palace if Itaru could not reach him in time. He pressed the button to fold his tamiken back to a single grip. Okubo was just steps away from the gates. Desperately, he hurled the folded tamiken at the duke. The projectile sailed through the air and struck Okubo in the back of the head. The duke fell to the ground, limbs splayed in all directions.

Itaru was on him in moments. He snatched his blade from the ground and unsheathed it, cutting fast and hard.

Okubo rolled, taking Itaru's blow on his blade and shoving back. He leaped to his feet. The old duke fought with fury. Itaru struggled to find an opportunity for counterattack, besieged by Okubo's swift, fierce blows. He feared for his life before not the aging duke but the samurai general he had seen from afar decades ago. Itaru was seventeen years old again on Mt. Enodake, scrabbling for his life against impossible odds.

No, I am not that child. He shifted his sword grip, ducked another slash, and pressed the attack. Their swords sang, glancing off each other again and again. He forgot the battle behind him. There was only the present, the passion of conflict.

He and Okubo traded blows, but neither could gain an advantage. Itaru slipped. His weary body couldn't recover quickly enough. Okubo slashed at his neck, and Itaru jerked back. Fire lanced across his throat.

He touched his neck. Only a glancing blow. A tenth of a second slower and his blood would have been spilled all over the bridge. *I can't keep this up.* Okubo was not as fast as a droid, but he was skilled and inventive—unpredictable. And Itaru was tiring.

Okubo saw his fear, his doubt. "You're protecting heartless machines," he said between heaving breaths. "They killed your son."

"*Criminals* killed my son, not jinzou." A snarl left Itaru's throat as he attacked again. His second wind was more furious than the first. He moved as fast as a droid, twirling from blow to blow, never stopping or setting up a strike. Okubo met every attack with a counterattack of his own, unfazed.

Itaru feinted right and lunged, but Okubo was ready. The duke knocked Itaru's blade down and sliced across his chest. Itaru's legs buckled, and he stumbled.

Okubo slashed Itaru's side without hesitation. Pain hit Itaru like a hammer.

Blood spurted. He cried out, vainly holding the bleeding gash with his off-hand.

"Mugen could have lived." Okubo's eyes were wide, manic. "It was a mistake to trust them. You'd put our trust in them again."

"No." Itaru was beaten. His life ebbed onto the bridge. "I put our trust in us."

With the last of his strength, he leaped forward. Okubo raised his sword to finish him, bringing his blade down hard to overcome Itaru's weak block. Itaru didn't block, however. Okubo's sword cut deeply into Itaru's shoulder, and Itaru's blade slid into the duke's chest.

They collapsed. Their blood pooled, mixing in the cracks between the stones.

"You . . ." Okubo spoke with difficulty, gasping for each breath. "Fool . . . she . . . will . . . kill . . . "

"How is that different"—Itaru winced with his own pain, his death as certain as Okubo's—"from what we do to each other? They are like us. They want . . . to live."

Okubo Toshimichi tilted back his head. He gazed at the sky. His last breath was gone.

"Papa!" Kano floated at his side. "Papa, no!"

He touched Kano's cheek with a trembling hand and smiled. "It's a warrior's death."

"Baka," she said, a tear running down her cheek. "What about us?"

"I'm sorry. For everything. I wasted—"

"That's him!" cried a journalist. The crowd followed behind him. "He's the one who destroyed Izanami!"

They closed in. The sky darkened.

"Kuso," Kano muttered. "I'll handle this." She stood preparing to address the crowd when a shadow fell across them all.

Kano gasped and bowed. The crowd bowed as well, even the journalist who had accused him, as the emperor's palanquin trundled over to them.

Itaru would have bowed if he could. It didn't matter. He had accomplished what he came for. What was one more dishonor?

The crowd gasped as the curtains opened. Several human guards hurried to put themselves between the crowd and the exposed emperor—several were wounded and bleeding, but they knew their duty.

The emperor stepped down from the mechanical palanquin. He was a little older than Itaru and dressed in a simple cotton shirt buttoned up the center to a high collar at his neck. His moustache and goatee were groomed to three sharp points. He walked straight-backed with two swords on his belt—mortal laws did not apply to the Son of Heaven.

"Shimada Itaru." He spoke softly, but his voice carried as far as the main road. It came from the palanquin, Itaru realized. Somehow the machine picked up and amplified his words. "Did you destroy Izanami, the Daughter of Japan?"

Itaru was too weak to lie or even sit up. His bones ached against the hard ground, but he didn't mind. Peace washed over him. "Yes, Your Majesty. I thought"—he took a shuddering breath—"to save Japan. She is aware, Your Majesty. All the jinzou are." He said it not for the emperor, who already knew, but for the crowd. Those who heard him clutched their hearts.

Itaru committed treason by revealing a secret the emperor had wanted hidden, but it was better that they knew. "She lied to us. To me. And I thought . . . she had killed my son." His voice rose to a crack. He swallowed. "I was wrong, though. I am at your mercy."

The emperor's face was as impassive as a jinzou's. "Can you sit?" he said.

Itaru shook his head.

The emperor gestured to someone behind him. Itaru's perception of time blurred. He was aware of movement and nothing else, and then, he was kneeling on a reed mat there on the bridge, held up on either side by imperial servants—a human on one side, one of the giant jinzou on the other. Each bowed their face to the ground, holding one of Itaru's arms firmly near the shoulder so he would not fall.

"Shimada Itaru. You have destroyed the Daughter of Japan." The emperor's voice boomed over the waters. He loomed over Itaru, one hand on his scabbard and the other on the hilt of his blade. Itaru suddenly wondered how the emperor knew his name. "You have also saved the Son of Heaven, exposed a traitor, and enlightened us all. It is beyond even my power to save your life, but I grant you the honor of seppuku. I will act as your second if you will have me."

Itaru no longer had energy for words. His head bobbled in a clumsy nod.

The sky shone a brilliant white with blue at the edges. He was no longer aware of the crowd or even those holding his arms. He was only barely aware of the emperor. A fading part of him knew he had been granted a great honor, but the greater joy still was that he would join Mugen and, finally, be at peace.

And then he was.

13

Haikei, Sensei Sakakura.

Thank you for your letter. I am glad that all has been well with you since I left the shop. The zaibatsu also speak well of you. I have even heard that your name once crossed the lips of the emperor himself. I am proud that my former sensei should be spoken of so highly.

Below is a transcription of the interview you asked about. Some of the details are fictitious gyufun, of course. His Majesty and the Council are quite strict about what the public needs to know. I slipped the truth in here and there, however. I hope you can read the air and understand.

Despite the desire for secrecy, I believe the emperor is acting with the best intentions toward Japan. When I was told some of my answers would be changed for the sake of the nation, I received a note from His Majesty with the words, "Forgive me."

Ironically, those were also her first words to me after she had been reactivated.
Please give my regards to your new apprentice.

Keigu,
Shimada Kano
Vice Minister of Technology

The Ministry of Technology has been the center of focus in Japan for decades but never more than in the past year. We had a chance to sit down briefly with the newly decorated vice minister, Shimada Kano, to talk about what's been going on behind ministry doors and what we can expect from the future.

INDUSTRIAL JOURNAL: Shimada-san, thank you for this opportunity. I hope you are well.
SHIMADA KANO: I am, thank you, Hana-san.

IJ: I don't want to waste too much of your time, so I'll get right to the questions our readers have been asking. First, tell us about what you found in the basement of the ministry last month.

SHIMADA: As you know, we've been sorting through the wreckage for some time—not just Izanami's debris but also that of other dismantled droids underneath the ministry, from the Meganebashi Incident, and elsewhere. What we've found confirms what His Divine Majesty told us after Meganebashi: the jinzou are in contact with each other, of course, but—

IJ: But not aware?

SHIMADA: No.

IJ: Yet you've found something new. Tell us about that.

SHIMADA: *(Sits up excitedly.)* We uncovered a copy of her core—Izanami's central "personality," if you will. We believe it was downloaded automatically, perhaps at the first sign of danger. We have been working day and night, and we hope to have her—the true Izanami, rather than the infant machine we've been using in her absence—back on-the-line within a week or two.

IJ: That is exciting. Will she have lost anything from the incident?

SHIMADA: It's still too early to say, but her evolutionary programming means that she should be able to regain anything she has lost relatively quickly. She learns rapidly, even more so through her connections with the other jinzou.

IJ: That is great news. If you don't mind, I'd like to go back to something you touched on earlier. The jinzou—and Izanami herself—aren't aware at all, is that correct?

SHIMADA: That is correct.

IJ: Yet wasn't it your father who claimed that they were? He was involved in the—

SHIMADA: The Meganebashi Incident, yes. He saved the emperor's life.

IJ: And also murdered Duke Okubo and destroyed Izanami as well. Do you think he was insane? Or did he know something that we don't?

SHIMADA: His Majesty has already spoken to this many times. He was in close touch with the ministry as you know. He knew she had been destroyed before even *your* people did. If the jinzou were aware, His Majesty would be among the first to know. It would be his duty to inform Japan.

IJ: So you believe your father was wrong, then. Is insanity the only explanation?

SHIMADA: *(Pauses.)* The man I knew was wise, clever, and good. He raised my brother and me after we lost our mother to cholera. But I . . . I regret that I cannot explain all of his actions at the end. The man who gave his life to protect the Son of Heaven? *That* is my father.

IJ: Of course. You honor him deeply. One last question before you return to your most important work. Suppose the jinzou really were aware or became aware at some future point if that were possible. *Could* there be a danger?

SHIMADA: Duke Okubo-sama believed there was a danger. He believed it so much that he killed in an effort to avoid it. I cannot say what will become of jinzou and humans or whether there is a danger. But I do know that the fear of danger can be more dangerous than the threat itself. We cannot always predict or prevent danger, Hana-san, but we *can* create it from nothing.

IJ: A fascinating view. Thank you, Shimada-san. We appreciate your thoughts and your time.

{}

Adam Heine *lives in Thailand where he and his wife foster kids with nowhere to go (current value: ten kids; current status: only mostly insane). He spends a lot of time training these kids to be gamers, thinkers, and supervillains. (Though a few insist on being good at sports and stuff, he tries not to hinder them.)*

By day, Adam is the Design Lead for the upcoming computer roleplaying game Torment: Tides of Numenera. *By night, he writes science fiction and fantasy for whomever will pay him. His short stories have appeared in* Beneath Ceaseless Skies, Paizo's *Pathfinder Tales, and the anthology* Tomorrow's Cthulhu. *You can see more of what he's written and what he's working on at adamheine.com.*

He desperately tries to pretend that he still has spare time in which to watch Daredevil *and play the latest* Shadowrun.

CPSIA information can be obtained
at www.ICGtesting.com
Printed in the USA
LVOW12s0345170516

488457LV00007B/9/P